ELEVEN, TWELVE ... DIG AND DELVE

REBEKKA FRANCK BOOK 6

WILLOW ROSE

Copyright Willow Rose 2015
Published by Jan Sigetty Boeje
All rights reserved.

No part of this book may be reproduced, scanned, or distributed in any printed or electronic form without permission from the author.

This is a work of fiction. Any resemblance of characters to actual persons, living or dead is purely coincidental. The Author holds exclusive rights to this work. Unauthorized duplication is prohibited.

Special thanks to my editor Jean Pacillo
http://www.ebookeditingpro.com

Cover design by Juan Villar Padron,
https://juanjjpadron.wixsite.com/juanpadron

Follow Willow Rose on BookBub:
https://www.bookbub.com/authors/willow-rose

Connect with Willow Rose:
willow-rose.net

Sinkhole
A sinkhole, also known as a sink, sink-hole, shakehole, swallet, swallow hole, or doline (...) a depression or hole in the ground caused by some form of collapse of the surface layer.

— FROM WIKIPEDIA, THE FREE ENCYCLOPEDIA

CONTENTS

Part I
DAY 1, OCTOBER 6TH 2014

Chapter 1	3
Chapter 2	7
Chapter 3	11
Chapter 4	14
Chapter 5	17
Chapter 6	20
Chapter 7	25
Chapter 8	28
Chapter 9	33
Chapter 10	35
Chapter 11	38
Chapter 12	41
Chapter 13	45
Chapter 14	48
Chapter 15	51
Chapter 16	55
Chapter 17	58
Chapter 18	61
Chapter 19	64
Chapter 20	67
Chapter 21	70
Chapter 22	73
Chapter 23	77
Chapter 24	81
Chapter 25	84
Chapter 26	87
Chapter 27	90
Chapter 28	93
Chapter 29	97
Chapter 30	100

Chapter 31	103
Chapter 32	107
Chapter 33	110
Chapter 34	113
Chapter 35	116
Chapter 36	120
Chapter 37	123

Part II
DAY 4, OCTOBER 9TH 2014

Chapter 38	129
Chapter 39	134
Chapter 40	137
Chapter 41	140
Chapter 42	143
Chapter 43	146
Chapter 44	149
Chapter 45	152
Chapter 46	155

Part III
DAY 11-12, OCTOBER 16TH -17TH 2014

Chapter 47	161
Chapter 48	164
Chapter 49	168
Chapter 50	171
Chapter 51	174
Chapter 52	177
Chapter 53	181
Chapter 54	184
Chapter 55	187
Chapter 56	190
Chapter 57	193
Chapter 58	196
Chapter 59	199
Chapter 60	202
Chapter 61	205
Chapter 62	209

| Chapter 63 | 212 |
| Chapter 64 | 215 |

Part IV
DAY 15, OCTOBER 20TH 2014

Chapter 65	221
Chapter 66	225
Chapter 67	230
Chapter 68	232

Part V
DAY 19, OCTOBER 24TH 2014

| Chapter 69 | 237 |

Afterword	241
Books by the Author	243
About the Author	247

HIT THE ROAD JACK- EXCERPT

Prologue	253
1. May 2012	255
2. May 2012	258
Part 1	260
3. January 2015	261
4. January 2015	266
5. April 1984	270
6. January 2015	273
7. January 2015	279
8. January 2015	284
9. April 1984	287
10. January 2015	290

| *Click Here To Order* | 295 |

I

DAY 1, OCTOBER 6TH 2014

THE COLLAPSE

1

It was one of those things no one could have expected, and from where he was standing Claus Frandsen couldn't have seen it coming, even if he knew in advance. It wasn't something anyone felt or even suspected could happen in the neighborhood, especially since it was such a *nice* neighborhood. It was one of those that had a great school within walking distance, one where the owner's association made sure people's hedges met the right requirements and never became too high or too low, one of those that every year arranged a Christmas banquet at the community center, where most of them would attend and bring a dish. The kind of neighborhood where your children could play in the cul-de-sac without you having to keep a constant eye on them. It was a neighborhood where young people would settle, have their children, and then grow old there. They rarely left. It wasn't a particularly expensive neighborhood, just a really good one with good and decent people.

At least that's what they all thought it was. Until it happened. Until this thing happened that changed everything, even the people. Some would later say it brought out their true colors...that the disaster brought out their true nature.

Claus Frandsen from number ten was walking out his front door to get the newspaper. His dog Fifi, a small and, according to the neighbors often too loudly (but they would never tell him) barking poodle, tagged along with him. It had finally stopped raining after days of heavy rainfall. He was wearing his bathrobe over his PJ's that his wife had ironed so neatly the day before, but were now all wrinkled up after a long night of sleep.

Claus Frandsen was whistling. He wasn't usually a particularly happy or positive man, but this day was different. This morning, he had finally managed to persuade his wife, Ana, to let him have that motorcycle he had always dreamed about. Now that he was retired, he thought it was about time he realized his dreams.

"But I want to travel," his wife had said, once he had aired the idea for the first time.

"Then let's travel on my bike," Claus had argued.

"I'm not going anywhere on a thing like that," she said.

And that had been the end of that discussion so far. Until this morning, when she had finally caved in. She had rolled over to his side of the bed and looked into his eyes with a look Claus knew only meant that she wanted something from him.

"If I let you have a bike, will you buy me a house in Greece where we can go for three months every summer? Just like the Jespersens have?"

It was an expensive deal, but well worth it, Claus had thought. Now as he was whistling and walking to pick up the paper, he felt very satisfied with the deal. It was only too bad that he wouldn't be able to bring his bike with him to Greece every summer. It was, after all, in the summertime that it was best to ride a bike. The rest of the year it was cold, well it was cold for the most part in Denmark, but if you were lucky you could get a month or maybe three good weeks in July or August.

We should go in the winter instead, he thought to himself as he opened the mailbox and pulled out his newspaper. The headlines talked about the growing tension between Russia and Ukraine, about the possibility of a war in Europe again.

Claus Frandsen scoffed. *Had history taught them nothing?* All this aggression led to nowhere. Everybody always ended up as losers in war. Claus should know. After spending years trying to help clean up the mess they made in the former Yugoslavia in the early nineties, as the Commander in Chief for the Danish Battalion, he'd seen his share of atrocities and heard a lot of stories that didn't need to be told again.

When will they ever learn?

Fifi barked and he petted her on the top of her curly head. It was Ana's dog, but he had kind of grown to like her over time.

"Yes, Fifi, I know you're anxious to get your breakfast and, frankly, so am I," he said.

The two of them started walking back towards the house as Claus spotted his neighbor from number twelve, Mrs. Sigumfeldt. She was walking to her car, followed by her three little munchkins, ages six, eleven, and twelve.

"Good morning," he chirped and waved. "It's going to be a beautiful one."

Mrs. Sigumfeldt shooed her children into the station wagon one after the other, then waved back.

"We'll have to see about that, Mr. Frandsen. Looks like it won't stay dry all day. Got them big dark clouds coming at us again. Enjoy your day."

"You too."

Fifi barked like she wanted in on the conversation, but

Mrs. Sigumfeldt had already closed the door and started the engine.

Claus Frandsen called her towards the door and opened it for the small dog. "Come on, Fifi. Let's go get breakfast."

The two of them had about fifty seconds more to live.

2

MRS. SIGUMFELDT WAS late, as usual. In the back seat of her minivan, the kids were arguing—also as usual. As a matter of fact, everything seemed to be just as usual, and it might as well have been, if it hadn't been for the disaster luring underneath the road on which she was driving.

She couldn't hear it because of the kids quarreling inside the car, but underneath the wheels of her Kia minivan, the ground was crackling, some would later in interviews on live TV refer to it as the ground sighing; others would say they had noticed a wailing rumble in the distance, like the ground was weeping. If that was true or just something they made up because they wanted to be on TV, no one would ever know.

"Could you please just settle your differences?" Mrs. Sigumfeldt said, diplomatically and emotionlessly to her children in the back. She didn't even bother to get really upset with them anymore. The arguing went on, day after day, hour after hour, and she had learned to block it out, to simply stop caring in order to survive.

They didn't hear her and kept arguing. It was the oldest, Jacob, and her middle child (always the troublemaker), Christian, who were discussing something, and had been all morning. Mrs. Sigumfeldt had no idea what the discussion was all about, but she seldom did. She rarely cared enough. It might have been a Minecraft discussion, it might not. At that point, she didn't care anymore. She was late for her work as a lawyer at Morch & Partners, a highly esteemed law firm where they expected her to arrive early and leave late, if she wanted to keep her position, for which there were *hundreds of applicants out there just as experienced as her that would kill for her job if she didn't want it.* (Her boss, the company's senior partner Mr. Morch never hesitated to tell her when he wasn't satisfied with her work-ambition, as he liked to put it.)

Mrs. Sigumfeldt looked at her cellphone and checked her emails while driving down the street of Blegevej in the nice neighborhood in Stoholm outside of Viborg. She grumbled when she noticed an email she was supposed to have answered on Friday, before the weekend. Now, Mr. Morch was going to have a fit.

Oh, how she loathed Mondays.

"Mom! Watch out!" Jacob screamed from the back seat.

Mrs. Sigumfeldt looked up just in time to spot the car approaching from the side, just in time to avoid it crashing into her. She lost control of the car and hit the brakes, causing the tires to squeal. The car skidded sideways and ended in the hedge of Mr. and Mrs. Bjerrehus in number six, who had invited the Sigumfeldts for dinner once, but never again after their boys broke their very expensive Ming-vase bought for twelve thousand kroner on auction in Viborg.

Mrs. Sigumfeldt screamed as the car slid sideways into the bush and the airbags were deployed.

"Is everyone alright?"

The door to the car was opened and a woman looked inside. "I'm so so sorry. I didn't see you."

Mrs. Sigumfeldt pushed herself free from the airbag and stumbled outside. "Are you alright?" the woman asked again.

Mrs. Sigumfeldt grumbled, annoyed, and blinked her eyes to better focus. "Oh, it's you," she said.

The woman that had hit them in her Toyota Corolla was Mrs. Jansen from number five across the street. It was well known in the neighborhood that her husband, Mr. Jansen, who was a truck driver, was beating her. To cope with the abuse, Mrs. Jansen, a nurse at the hospital in Viborg, numbed herself with strong sedatives that she stole from the hospital and flushed them down with cheap gin.

Usually, Mrs. Sigumfeldt, like everyone else in the neighborhood, had the highest amount of sympathy for the poor Mrs. Jansen, well, except when she was crying and screaming like a crazy person in the street at night and ringing their doorbells, drunk and high on pills. But her goodwill towards her and empathy for her situation disappeared right at that moment.

"My children!" Mrs. Sigumfeldt said, and pushed Mrs. Jansen aside. She pulled the back door open and looked inside the car.

Six eyes looked back at her, and she breathed with relief. "Is everyone alright?" she asked.

All of them nodded. Their eyes were wide and anxious. There was no blood, no bruises. They were all in their seats still. *Shaken, but not stirred*, Mrs. Sigumfeldt thought to herself. She didn't know why. This was hardly the time for witty comments.

Mrs. Sigumfeldt looked at her youngest boy, Frederic. "Did anyone get hurt?" she asked.

They all shook their heads. "We're alright, Mom," her oldest, Jacob, said. "Just shocked, that's all."

"Mommy?" Frederic said.

"Yes, sweetie. Are you okay?"

He swallowed hard, and then reached out his arms towards her. She took off his seatbelt and held him in her arms. "I was scared, Mommy."

"I know. It's okay," she said, and stroked his hair. "You're fine. It could have been really bad, but it wasn't. We're all fine."

3

IN NUMBER SEVEN, David Busck was sitting on the bed. It was his brother's house. His feet were on the wooden floor, his elbows leaning on his knees, his face hidden between his hands.

It was morning once again, and David hated those more than anything. A new day was beginning, the sun rising on the horizon. David couldn't see it, since he hadn't bothered to pull away the curtains. In the kitchen, he could hear his brother and his wife talking. Their four-month old baby was crying. Once again, they were probably discussing whether David would get out of bed today or not.

He couldn't blame them.

He had lost track of the days, but it was more than two weeks he had spent in this room that was one day supposed to be the nursery. They had taken David in when he needed it the most, and for that, he was eternally grateful.

David sighed and looked at the gun on the table by the bed. They didn't know he had it. No one knew. He had bought it once he returned to Denmark…from some guy on the streets of Copenhagen. He didn't care that it was illegal. That was before his brother asked him to come to Jutland and live at his house until things got better. Till everything settled down a little.

So far, they had only gotten worse.

He hadn't bought the gun for his protection. He knew that he was safe now that he was back in his old fairy-tale country, where people could walk the streets safely and where a journalist could report his stories freely.

The gun was for himself.

David picked it up and felt its weight. A tear left his eye and rolled across his cheek when he thought about all the times they had held a gun just like it to his head, yelling and screaming at him. Then they called his family on Skype and told them they would shoot him if they didn't bring them the money.

He still remembered his mother's screams and cries. She hadn't been herself since, either. None of them had.

"Why did you have to go anyway?" his father had yelled at him, once he had landed and set foot on Danish soil. They had taken him back to their house, sneaking him out of the airport, with a little help from the police, to avoid the many reporters and photographers waiting for him at the arrival gate.

"Do you have any idea what you've put us through? Your mother is a wreck."

"I'm sorry," was all he could say. And he really was sorry. He felt truly guilty for ending up in this situation. For causing all this distress to his own family. Unlike most of the journalists who went to Syria to cover the war, he didn't have a big TV station or a newspaper sending him there. No, he had gone on his own. As a freelancer. He had followed two Danish kids travelling from Denmark to become holy warriors in a war that had nothing to do with them. He thought it was an important story to tell. That was how he worked. That was what he did. But his father was right. He didn't have to go. It was entirely his own fault that he was captured.

He couldn't blame his father for being angry.

"Do you have any idea what we had to do? Three million dollars. That's how much money they wanted. We had to sell everything. We had to ask the bank to help us; we had to ask all of our friends for charity. Do you have any idea how humiliating it is to have to beg your friends for money?"

"Mogens, don't," his mother had said. "The important thing is that he's back. He's safe. It's all that matters now."

That was the part that had hurt David the most. The look in his mother's eyes. The pain, the hurt that he had caused her could still make him cry while sitting alone in the room in his brother's house.

David's hand was shaking heavily as he lifted up the gun and put it in his mouth. It felt cold on his tongue. David was sweating and crying as he said goodbye to this cruel world and moved his finger to pull the trigger.

4

MARTIN BUSCK HEARD the loud sound coming from his brother's room and looked at his wife.

"What was that?"

She looked at him with anxious eyes. They were both so concerned about David and his state of mind ever since he'd returned from Syria, where he spent ninety days in captivity. He hadn't been well. They all knew it, but no one knew what to do. All he wanted was for them to leave him alone, he said. There was no way Martin would ever leave his beloved baby brother alone. He loved him way too much for that. Yes, he had been stupid for traveling into a dangerous war-zone like that on his own, but Martin understood him. He knew he had only followed his passion...to tell the important stories that no one else did. And Martin admired him for that. It wasn't sensible, it wasn't smart, it wasn't a choice Martin would ever make, but still he respected his brother's choice. Martin's wife, Mathilde had been amazing through the process. She hadn't even been angry at the fact that they had been forced to sell their house in Aarhus to help pay for his release. They were now deeply in debt, and would never be able to pay it off for the rest of their lives, based on the living they made.

Still, Mathilde never said a word.

"Do what you have to do," she had said when Martin had told her.

He had never loved her more.

"Go see!" Mathilde said. The baby was crying in her arms.

Martin's heart was in his throat as he rushed towards the door to David's room. Many pictures flickered through his mind of what might have happened. He knew David was fragile. He knew he didn't sleep at night and that he dreaded the day.

What have you done, baby brother?

Martin imagined a whole lot of things as he opened the door to his brother's room, but he could never have imagined what he saw.

The entire room had sunk into the ground. The bed was sticking up in the middle of it; the dresser was slowly being pulled down.

And so was David.

"HEEELP!"

David hollered and screamed while being pulled down into the huge hole. "Help me. Help me!"

Martin jumped inside the hole and grabbed David's hand. He was still being pulled into the middle of it. Everything around him was sinking, disappearing into a vast darkness underneath.

Martin held onto his brother's hand, screaming, pulling it. But his hand was slippery. It was slowly sliding out of Martin's grip.

"No!" Martin yelled. "Hold on, baby brother. Hold on to me. Don't let go!"

The force pulling David was strong. The two brothers stared into each other's eyes, thinking of all the times they had spent together, all the fights they had, all the pranks they had pulled, all the things they had gone through and survived.

Was this the way they were supposed to say goodbye?

No, dear God. Not like this. Please. Don't let the ground swallow him!

Voices were screaming behind Martin and he felt hands on his shoulders as someone tried to pull him up. David's hand slipped further, and now they were only holding on by their fingertips.

"NO!" Martin screamed.

"Help!" David said, half-choked as his fingers finally let go, and the hole sucked him down with a large slurping sound, along with the desk, the dresser, and the bed.

"NOOOOOO!"

Martin screamed as a set of strong hands pulled him backwards, hands he would later learn belonged to his neighbor from across the street in number six, Mr. Bjerrehus, who had been walking his dog in the street when he heard the screams coming from inside the house.

5

Afrim Berisha from number four kissed his mother at the door, then sprang for his bike when Buster, his Golden Retriever, came running for him in the yard.

"I'm sorry, buddy," he said. "You can't come. You know they won't let dogs inside the school."

Buster answered with a loud bark. Afrim heard the school bell ring. He was late. There was nothing unusual about that. His school was a small school with only fifty students. One of Denmark's smallest, they said. All were local kids living in the neighborhood or just outside of it. There had been talk of closing the school, Afrim had heard his mother say, but so far it had survived. Afrim hoped it would be closed, so he wouldn't have to go to school ever again. He didn't like school, and would much rather play with Buster all day and ride his bike. In that sense, Afrim was just a normal eight-year old boy.

"I'm late, buddy."

Afrim was a neighbor to the school, yet always the last kid to arrive in the classroom.

Today, he wasn't going to school at all.

He had pulled the bike through the yard and out on the other side of the fence when he heard tires squeal and turned his head to see Mrs. Sigumfeldt, who lived further down the street and whose boys were always bullying Afrim, just avoid being hit by Mrs. Jansen, the lady whose eyes were always foggy and who walked funny and always bumped into things and got bruises on her face.

"That was a close one," he mumbled, as he watched Mrs. Sigumfeldt jump out of the car and Mrs. Jansen tell her how sorry she was.

The car had ended up in Mr. Bjerrehus' hedge, and Afrim knew they would get in trouble for that. Mrs. Bjerrehus took very good care of her yard, and she liked the hedge because it kept people's curious eyes out. What Mrs. Bjerrehus didn't know was that Afrim could look into her yard from his room upstairs and see her as she walked around naked in her yard. He thought the world should be glad that Mrs. Bjerrehus took good care of her hedge.

Buster barked again, this time louder and much more insistent, when Afrim suddenly felt the ground rumble under his feet. Growing up in Albania, his father had known about earthquakes and told Afrim about them, and now Afrim wondered if this could be one. If this was how an earthquake felt. Only, he knew from his father that there were no earthquakes in Denmark. Denmark's underground was all limestone. There were no mountains and, therefore, no quakes.

Afrim heard another sound and turned just in time to see a part of the school disappear into a huge hole in the ground. The building simply sank. Afrim stared at the hole it left where the school library used to be. He looked at Buster, then threw his bike on the ground and started running towards the house.

"MOOOM!"

Behind him, the street opened up and swallowed a car

driving by, along with Mrs. Sigumfeldt, her kids, Mrs. Jansen and Mrs. Bjerrehus's entire hedge.

Afrim and Buster sprang for their lives as the ground fell into the hole behind them faster than they could sprint.

They barely made it to the front door before the ground rumbled again and their yellow house came down in front of Afrim.

He shrieked.

"Mom? MOOOOM?"

The ground shook again, and Afrim fell; he grabbed onto Buster as the soil opened up underneath them and started pulling them down forcefully. Afrim held on to Buster with all his strength as they fell and fell into the deep massive darkness.

6

In number three, Thomas Soe was staring at the white blank page on his screen. He wiped his sweaty palms off on his pants and sipped more coffee. He had been staring at the blank page all night, wondering when inspiration would come.

On the bed next to him lay the girl. She was whimpering and sobbing behind the gag. Thomas couldn't focus.

"Could you be quiet for just a second!" he said to her.

The girl answered with another whimper. He looked at her. He blinked his eyes a couple of times to make sure she was real. Thomas never knew what was real and what wasn't these days.

Stay calm, Thomas, he heard his late mother's voice say. *You'll lose control. You're losing touch with reality, my son.*

He had thought the girl would give him the inspiration he needed, that he longed for so badly. But he had been staring at the blank page all night without being able to put down as much as a word.

The girl didn't help much.

Maybe she needs a little motivation.

The way he remembered it, he had picked her up last night in Viborg, the closest big city to where he lived. She had been waiting for the bus on a street somewhere. She'd probably visited some friend and was on her way back home. Thomas didn't even bother to ask. He had simply driven by her and rolled down the window, showing off one of his handsome smiles.

"Need a ride?"

The girl was no more than sixteen, he would guess. He liked them at that age. The girl had said no thank you at first, but Thomas had insisted.

"Come on. I'm going that way anyway. I promise to be nice. Come on. It's raining. You'll catch a cold."

The fact that he was only twenty-four helped seal the deal, along with the fact that he was a famous writer, a poet who had written a work at the age of only eighteen that had everyone talking about him. The newspapers called him the artist of the century and said his poems were explosive and that they were renewing the genre of poetry by adding the horror, and having blood dripping from every line and word. *It's like the entire book is burning between your hands,* one reviewer wrote.

"Haven't I seen you somewhere before?" the girl had asked.

"You got me," Thomas had said, smiling again. "Don't tell anyone."

The fact that he was a celebrity had made her change her mind instantaneously. He could tell by the look in her eyes and her sudden giggle.

"You're that writer, aren't you? That poet?"

"Guilty as charged."

"You wrote those poems that everyone is talking about… where you pretend to be molesting your girlfriend. We read some of them in class. I loved them. The way you declare your love for her and describe your pain by imagining you hurt her. Because she hurt you, right? The axe is a metaphor for your anger."

"If you say so."

"My teacher told us that. I'm not really good with the whole analyzing-a-poem thing. But with yours, I could really identify with the pain. I could relate."

"That's splendid. You're getting wet."

The girl giggled again, then made her final decision. She ran to the door and got in the passenger seat. Thomas smiled and drove off, thinking, finally, he would be able to write again.

But he was wrong. Even though he had tied her down like he believed he had done to his ex-girlfriend six years ago, and even though he had beat her up in anger and hurt, feeling the frustration of being rejected all over again, he hadn't been able to write a word yet. Not one single word.

And it was all her fault.

Maybe she needed to hurt a little more. Seeing her in pain made him feel better. With Rikke, his ex-girlfriend, he had written the poems first, while she was still in pain. And then he had killed her. First, he had imagined what it would be like to kill her with her father's axe; he had imagined every little detail of how it would be and written it down in his poems. Then, he read them to her. He read every poem, every word of it out loud and watched how her eyes pleaded for him to let her go.

Then he had killed her. It had been a thing of beauty. Like fireworks in his mind. The girl he had known since they were nine year's old. The girl he had dated for three years before she tore his heart to pieces. Before he responded by chopping her into pieces. At least he thought he had. He wasn't sure. As a matter of fact, he wasn't sure about anything lately. He had a way of getting lost in his daydreams. He could imagine the strangest things simply while walking down the street.

Suddenly, people's faces passing him would turn bloody and arms and limbs would fall off. Then he would blink his eyes and everything would turn back to normal. And it could happen out of the blue. Thomas could be talking to someone, then start imagining that he stabbed the person with a knife, cut him or her open, and watched the blood spurt out. Then, a second later, it would be gone and the person was still talking.

Once his ex-girlfriend went missing, the police had, of course, asked questions afterwards. Who could blame them after the poems were published? But no one in their right mind believed that the most famous poet in the country could really be a killer. A little disturbed, maybe, but he was an artist. Artists were allowed to be quirky, even a little mad. They had to be. And there was never a body. Only a missing person's report. Her own father ended up taking the fall when they found the bloody axe in his garage with his fingerprints on it and the DNA that determined that the blood belonged to Rikke. Thomas wasn't sure if he had dreamt it, but he thought he remembered placing the axe back in the garage. It could have been a dream. It might have been. He would never know. But he thought Rikke would be happy that her dad finally got what he deserved for treating Rikke like he did, the drunk.

"It was all for you, my love," he whispered out in the darkness of his room with the heavy curtains pulled to keep the world out. He had bought the house on the quiet street outside of Viborg to get some peace for his writing. And to get away from people and his many strange images.

Thomas looked at the girl on the bed. She seemed to be real. He couldn't remember her name. But it didn't matter. He slapped her across the face. The girl cried. Thomas slapped her again. She was definitely real. But, then again, maybe not. He had been tricked before. It was right after Rikke had broken up with him, telling him she was now with Jon, a super pumped guy who worked out at her gym. That was when the many visions started. It began with him imagining all the things he would like to do to Rikke. Once she was gone, he started seeing many other bloody girls in his house. Some would fall out of his closet when he opened it, others would be in his bathtub when he went in the bathroom, soaking in bloody water. He never knew if they were really there or not. Sometimes, he remembered hurting them; other times, he didn't.

The girl whimpered again, and Thomas stared at her. Blood was running from her nose. Thomas wiped it off and smelled the napkin afterwards. Then he slapped her again. He still wasn't sure if she was real or if he had imagined picking her up. The girl tried to scream.

This first Monday in October got off to a bad start for many of the people in the small neighborhood on Blegevej, but only few had it as awful as this girl.

7

MALENE PEDERSEN WAS screaming behind her gag, but nothing but muffled sounds came out into the dark room.

He's crazy. I gotta get out of here somehow before he kills me.

The man she knew as the famous poet had that look in his eyes again. Those black eyes were flooding with fury. He was biting his lip while watching her between slaps. When he stopped biting himself, his teeth left a mark. Malene's body was hurting from all the beating.

How had she gotten herself into this? How could she have been so stupid to get into a car with this guy? Wasn't this what her mother had always warned her about? How could she have been so stupid? Stupid!

Malene sobbed, feeling sorry for herself, while the poet stared at her and kept talking to her like she was someone else.

"Why did you do it?" he asked. "Why did you have to hurt me like that?"

Malene didn't understand. She tried to talk, but couldn't because of the gag. What did he want from her? He hadn't raped her as she thought he would. What was he going to do to her? She had been asking herself that question all night, while waiting for him to make his move. Was there any way she could get out of here alive? She didn't even know where she was. As soon as she had gotten into the car last night, he had slammed his fist into her face and she hadn't seen anything until she opened her eyes and found herself tied to this bed. He had beaten her, then sat by the computer staring at the blank page for hours. That scared her even more than the beating. His silence. The staring at the screen. He hadn't even written anything. Not a word.

"Why did you do it, you *bitch*!?" He now yelled at her and punched her in the stomach.

It blew the air out of Malene and she gasped behind the gag. She moaned in pain and cried heavily. Who could have thought that the country's most highly regarded writer was this insane?

Please, stop this. Please, someone stop this. Oh, God. Please. Don't let him hit me again. Don't let him kill me. I have so much to live for. I want to go home to my family. I want to see my mom again. I want to hold my baby brother. Please, do something. I don't care what it is. Just do something.

"I'm gonna teach you to never cheat on anyone again!" he yelled, then slammed his fist into her face once again.

Malene cried in pain. But as she was almost about to give up all hope, she felt something. The poet had tied her hands to the bed with a piece of rope, and now it seemed that she was able to move them a little more. She looked at the poet while he was yelling at her, telling her what a *liar* she was, what a *cheating bitch*, she was. *A whore*! Meanwhile, Malene was able to twist and squirm her wrists just enough to feel the rope loosen. The poet didn't seem to notice, and soon her arms were free. She was free. Quicker than he was able to react, she sat up and swung her fist into his face. He fell backwards from the blow, and Malene untied the belt that he had used to hold her feet together. While removing the gag, she jumped off the bed and started running, but the poet managed to grab her leg and pull her down. She screamed and landed face down on the wooden floor. She kicked him in the face, and he yelled and let go of her leg. Malene climbed to her knees, her body aching from the beating, and reached out for the door handle. She managed to open it and rush out into the kitchen, where suddenly she was grabbed around the waist and lifted into the air. She struggled and screamed. The poet laughed and threw her against the counter, knocking the air out of her. Then he laughed and picked her up again. She kicked him in the stomach, and he bent over with a moan. Then he dropped her to the floor. She got up and tried to run, but he kicked her in the back, and she flew across the floor and landed head first into the stove.

Please, God, let me get out of here before he kills me. Please, help me!

In the distance, the ground underneath the entire neighborhood was moaning, some called it weeping. But Malene never heard it. All she heard was the poet's scream as he grabbed her hair and pulled till her head slammed into the counter and she could taste blood.

He laughed again, and she could tell that he enjoyed it, the sick bastard. Malene moaned and blinked her eyes to better focus. Just as she was about to lose all hope again, just as the poet grabbed her by the hair and was about to hit her once again, the ground beneath them—*oh the horror*—opened up and they were sucked into its infinite obscurity.

Just as Malene thought the day couldn't get any worse, it did.

8

"So, where to?"

The taxi driver looked at me in the rear-view mirror as I got inside his car.

"The train station. My train leaves in half an hour."

"The train station it is," the taxi-driver said, and turned the car around in the small street.

I rolled the window down and waved to my friend, Lone, who was standing in the doorway of her house on Blegevej, number fourteen. She was still in her bathrobe. I had spent the weekend at her house while Sune took care of the kids alone back in Karrebaeksminde. I had missed them all like crazy. William had turned a year and a half, and it was the first time I had been away from him this long.

I couldn't wait to get back. Two days with my friend crying over her life was more than enough. I love Lone, that's not it; I just really looked forward to seeing my family again. It had been a depressing weekend. My friend was so devastated. I felt bad for her. Her husband had left a week ago, telling her he was fed up with everything, and using the d-word.

Divorce.

I hated that word. But nevertheless, it kept showing up more and more often in my circle of friends. It was just that time in our lives when people split up, I guess. We knew it when we got married, didn't we? That half of us would end up in divorce. Those were just the statistics, the coldhearted facts. In my friend Lone's case, there wasn't anything left to save, the way I saw it. They had both given up. She was a nurse and had slept with one of the doctors while on conference in Germany a couple of weeks ago. So, in that sense, I didn't feel sorry for her, but it was still a horrible thing when it came to this. Once she told him about her little escapade, her husband also admitted to having slept with some woman from his office, so I guess it's true that it takes two to divorce.

"So, you were just visiting?" the driver asked, trying to make small talk.

"Yeah. I have an old friend from high school living here. I live in Karrebaeksminde. It's been awhile since we last saw each other."

"That's nice," he said. "That you keep in touch."

"Yeah, I guess it is kind of neat."

"And rare these days," he said.

"Well, Facebook makes it a lot easier," I said, and found my phone in my pocket. I looked at it. I had forgotten to charge it. Only twenty percent left.

Damn it! Well, I can charge it on the train.

It was my plan to get some work done on my way back. I had an article that was due the next day for my newspaper *The Zeeland Times* and I hadn't been able to write a word all weekend. My head was hurting slightly from all the red wine we drank while talking about her miserable marriage, but I had to ignore it.

I called Sune.

"Hey, babe."

"I'm in the taxi now, going to the station. If all goes well, I'll be in Karrebaeksminde around one o'clock. Could you pick me up?"

"Sure," he said. He worked as a photographer at the same newspaper as me. He had taken the day off and was now cleaning the house, he told me, after a weekend of fun and kids. Sune didn't look much like a family-man with his Mohawk and black make-up on his eyes, but he was. He was one of the best dads you could find. He had been amazing with William when we first had him. Changed every diaper he could, and enjoyed every moment of it. He had even taken a 'daddy-leave' for six weeks while I went back to work after my year of maternity leave was over.

My dad was feeling better. I believed having a new grandson had a lot to do with it. He had taken care of William when Sune went back to work, just for a couple of months, until I found the right daycare for William.

I enjoyed immensely getting back to work. I wasn't really much of a stay-at-home-mom. I got restless. A year was a long time. I had, of course, written a couple of articles for the paper here and there. They had ended up giving me a column where I wrote about anything I liked, mostly about baby stuff and so on. Once I got back, I lucked out and landed a great story about the famous writer Emma Frost, who was looking for her daughter who had disappeared near Karrebaeksminde after running a stolen car into someone and leaving him in a coma. It had turned out to be an amazing story. That was nearly six months ago. The summer had been slow on stories, so I needed something good soon.

"So, how's Lone?" Sune asked. I could hear William babbling in the background, and held the phone closer to my ear. I hated being away from him.

"She'll be fine. How's William?"

"Everything's fine here. The big ones are driving me nuts,

though. So glad to be able to send them off to school in a few minutes. I'll take William to his daycare later."

I chuckled. I knew Julie and Tobias, our children from earlier marriages, could be a little much. They loved each other, but ever since we had all moved in together, Julie and Tobias had started fighting over things. It had been a little hard on Julie with all the changes in her life. She was used to being alone with me, and suddenly she had to share me with not only Sune, but also William, and even Tobias. Tobias enjoyed having a mother figure in his life for the first time, and I tried hard to be one, with the result that Julie became really jealous of him and asked if I loved him more than her. I would have to spend some time with her alone once I got back, I thought to myself, while Sune explained this morning's fight.

"I mean, Julie hasn't been acting very nice towards me lately either," he continued, while the taxi slowed down.

"She's doing her best, Sune," I said, annoyed. I hated when he blamed her. After all, we grownups were subjecting her to all these changes. It wasn't easy for a child. "It'll get better. We knew there would be some sort of reaction from the kids."

The taxi came to a complete stop. "Why are we stopping?" I asked the driver.

"But Tobias isn't reacting nearly as badly as she is," Sune continued. I hardly listened. I was busy looking out the window to see why the driver had stopped in the middle of the street.

"He's no saint either," I said.

There seemed to be some people gathered in the street. Two cars were blocking the road.

"I can't get past them," the driver said with a shrug.

"I have a train to catch!" I said. "I can't be late."

One car was in the hedge, while another was parked across the street, blocking everything. The taxi driver got out.

"That might be, but he certainly isn't acting as bad as Julie," Sune continued. "She has been really bad. The things she says to me. You have to talk to her when you get back…I won't…"

"Hold on, sweetie," I said. "Listen. I have a situation to deal with here. We can't get past some cars that have been in an accident, I guess. I only have fifteen percent left on my phone. I'll charge it on the train, then call you, alright?"

I didn't wait for his answer before I hung up, put the phone in my pocket, and got out.

"Hey! Could you please move your cars? I have a train to catch," I said.

The two women turned just in time to look at me before the earth underneath us grumbled and, in a matter of seconds, collapsed.

9

Oh, my God, I'm sinking!!

I was. I was sinking and sliding into the giant hole that had split open underneath me. There wasn't anything I could do. There was nothing to hold on to. I was literally being sucked into the ground. It was like a big giant mouth had opened up and swallowed me. It was like Pinocchio being sucked into the whale's mouth...or like Dorothy inside the tornado. There was no fighting it. The force pulling me down was way too strong.

It happened so quickly, I don't believe I even had time to scream or panic. I tried desperately to grab out, to hold onto something, to do anything, but the ground around me was sliding. Everything was sliding...the cars, the dirt, the asphalt that was broken to pieces and being sucked down along with me. There was no place to put my feet, nothing to hold on to. The ground underneath kept sliding, and I kept thinking: *This is it. I'm going to die. I'm sliding into the ground and will never come back up again.*

There were things everywhere. And people. Arms tried to grab me and hold onto me, but were pulled away again. At one point, I saw the taxi falling, sliding down beside me. I saw people in the ground with me and, at one point, something hit me, twirled right at me, and I realized it was the taxi driver's arm. I recognized the sleeve. The further I slid down, the more stuff was in the ground with me. Pieces of wood, bricks, tiles, and I realized it wasn't just me being sucked down. It was the entire neighborhood.

Get up. Try to get up. Grab onto something!

I kept my face pointing upwards, but soon lost the sense of up and down. The light disappeared quickly, and then there was nothing but darkness. I found a branch from what I believed was a tree and held onto it, but it was sliding right down with me.

Help! Oh, God, please help me!

A hand grabbed me and held onto me. I had no idea who it belonged to, since all light was gone, and I couldn't see. I could hardly breathe either. My mouth was soon filled with dirt, and I gasped for air, feeling how the ground was closing in on me as we slid downwards. In the darkness that was closing in on me, I held onto the little hand that had grabbed me the best I could.

Oh, God. Where will we land?

10

When the sliding finally did stop, I didn't dare to move. Underneath my feet was mud. It felt soft and wet, and I couldn't stop wondering if I would fall further down if I moved. It didn't seem stable. I was still holding the little hand in mine, but had no idea who was at the other end. Carefully I felt it until I reached an arm. It was sticking out of the mud wall next to me.

Someone is stuck in the mud. You have to help. Do something!

But I was scared. Afraid that moving would make the hole deeper or make the ground cave underneath me. I was in a pocket of some sort. There was air in there. I couldn't see the top, but I could breathe.

I felt the hand in mine. The fingers moved.

That's it. Someone is alive in there and you have to do something. Someone might be suffocating. Even if it's the last thing you do...

"Oh, hell," I exclaimed, and then started digging in the thick dirt. In the darkness, I managed to dig out the arm and then pull it towards me. The dirt moved dangerously and some fell onto my head, causing me to gasp and panic slightly.

Then I pulled the arm again, while moving the dirt surrounding the body. Soon, I felt a head and some shoulders. I gasped for air, and then dug again, even though the ground underneath my feet was starting to shake. I heard a thud and stopped for a few seconds, then continued.

"Even if it's the last thing I do…"

I felt the body's shoulders and realized it had to belong to a child. That made me dig even more frantically till I finally managed to pull the entire body out and it landed on top of me. As it did, the ground underneath my feet caved again. With the small body on top of me I started sliding further down. I screamed, then landed on something. I opened my eyes in the darkness.

I'm not dead. I'm not dead yet.

There was air where I was. Muffled sounds came from underneath me, and I realized I was on top of somebody. The child was still on top of me. I couldn't move.

Another thud followed and the ground collapsed again. The three of us slid downwards.

Not again! When will this stop? Where will we end up? Will they ever find us down here?

A big crash, a thumb, dirt in my mouth, eyes and nose. We landed on something harder this time. There was no one on top of me anymore. The child was next to me. Where were we? It seemed bigger? Like there was more room. I coughed and moved. I spat out dirt.

"Stay still," a voice said next to me. I guessed it belonged to the body I landed on. It was a male voice. "We don't know if the ground is safe here either," he continued.

I couldn't stop thinking about the small hand I had held in mine and the small body I had pulled out from the dirt. Was the child alive? I leaned over and touched the body. It was lying next to me. I found the face and leaned over to hear if there was breathing. Everything was so terribly quiet for what felt like an eternity until suddenly I felt a small warm wind hit my face.

The child was alive!

I grabbed the small body in my arms and held it tight. It seemed to be about the size of Julie. Maybe a little smaller.

"I'll take care of you," I whispered. "If it's the last thing I do."

"Keep still," the male voice said again. "Please. Don't move."

I sat still without moving for a little while.

My phone!

I reached into my pocket with a pounding heart, wondering if it might have fallen out during the fall. It hadn't. It was still there. I pulled it out and pressed a button. The light from the display lit up around us, and I realized we were in a small cave somewhere, a pocket under the ground. And there was no way out. Thick walls of dirt surrounded us on all sides.

11

"You think it stopped?"

I shone the light on the man's face. He looked at me, then shrugged. "I have no idea. But let's stay still till we know more."

He was smeared in dirt and mud, but I could tell he was handsome. I had seen him somewhere before. I just couldn't recall where.

I lit up the face of the child I was holding. It was a little boy. He looked like he was asleep, but I guessed he was unconscious.

"Better save your battery," the man said. "We don't know how long we're going to be in here."

"I only have eight percent left. I guess you're right," I said, looking at the display. As I suspected, there was no reception. I looked at the dirt ceiling that had closed above us and wondered if it was going to fall on us anytime soon and suffocate us, or if it would stay. Then I wondered how deep down we had fallen and, finally, if anyone would ever be able to dig us out again.

Did they even know we were down here, alive?

I shut off the phone and put it back in my pocket.

"I'm Rebekka, by the way," I said.

"David," the man answered.

"David Busck, right?" I said, remembering all of a sudden where I had seen him before.

The man answered with a deep sigh.

"Can't even catch a break deep under ground, huh?" I said, remembering all the articles and many angry open letters to the papers stating that it was the guy's own fault that he had been kidnapped, because he went as a freelancer, because he had no idea what he had gotten himself into. I, for one, understood him completely. He had been onto a great story. I would have done the same. Probably.

"I guess not," he said.

"So, what do you suggest we do now?" I asked.

"There's nothing we can do. We have to wait till they start digging for us."

"But that could take hours. The hole might even cave again and we could sink in deeper!"

I felt the panic spread throughout my body. The idea that we were trapped underground like this made me claustrophobic. The catastrophic feeling of death closing in on you.

"We'll run out of air," I said.

"Probably," David answered.

"Can't we just try and dig our way back up?" I asked.

"Probably not a very good idea," David said. "The ceiling above might crash in and we'll get smashed by the many tons of dirt and debris on top of us."

"But how will they dig us out if we can't dig our way up?"

David didn't answer. He didn't have to. I knew. There was no chance in hell they would be able to dig us out.

But I wasn't ready to give up that easily. I had a family to get home to. And home I was going, no matter how. There had to be a way.

With my right hand, I started digging into the side of the cave, while holding onto the boy with my left. I had promised myself to not let go of him again, so I wasn't going to.

I scratched the dirt away little by little, using my fingernails. After having dug for a few minutes, I suddenly felt David crawl up next to me, and soon he dug his fingers into the dirt as well.

Even if it led to nowhere, at least it gave us something to do.

12

THOMAS SOE HAD no idea where he was. It was dark and he couldn't see anything. His entire body was hurting and he couldn't move.

What happened? I remember falling. I remember sliding down. I remember dirt everywhere.

Thomas coughed and spat out some dirt. His mouth felt so dry. He was very thirsty. Where was he? Was this just another of his daydreams?

Carefully, he reached into his pocket and found his Zippo-lighter that used to belong to his dad, inside his package of cigarettes. He lit it and looked around.

What was this place? Some sort of cave?

He looked up and saw where he had fallen through the dirt ceiling. The hole had closed and shut off one end of the tunnel that he was in. At least it looked like a tunnel. He wasn't sure.

Suddenly, he remembered. The girl! Had she been another dream?

Thomas heard someone moan and turned his head. It wasn't her. It was a young boy. He was stuck under what used to be a garden fountain in Mrs. Bjerrehus's front yard in number six. A monstrous baby angel in solid marble had landed on his leg, and it was bleeding. Thomas stared, paralyzed, at the boy.

"Help me," the boy moaned.

Thomas had no idea what to do. All he could think of was the girl. He had to find her. If she was real, she could tell. If she told on him, she could ruin everything. The boy groaned in pain.

"Please, Mr.?"

"I …" Thomas paused. He had to keep focus. When had he seen the girl last? In the kitchen. She had hurt her head. And then it happened. He was pulled into the ground and he didn't remember anything else but waking up in this strange cave that was just tall enough for him to stand up. What on earth had happened?

It's just a dream. You're losing touch with reality again, Thomas.

"Please Mr., please help?" the boy pleaded.

Thomas looked at him while biting his lip. The lighter was getting warm in his hand. Was the boy even real?

"Please? My foot is stuck."

Thomas knew the boy. Afrim was his name. He had heard his mother yell at him so often. They were Muslims. No one in the street ever talked to them much. They were never invited to the block parties. His mother wore one of those scarfs to cover up her hair. Thomas had never talked to them; he never really talked to anyone in the neighborhood. He liked to keep to himself. But he had seen the boy often. He lived across the street from Thomas in number four and rode his bike to school every morning, even though the school was his next-door neighbor.

Maybe the boy knew where the girl was? Maybe he had seen her?

Thomas kneeled next to Afrim. His face was smeared in dirt. So were his clothes.

"It's heavy," the boy said. "I can't get it off me."

Thomas put the lighter on the ground, then grabbed the marble angel and lifted it off the boy's leg. The boy pulled out and rolled away. Thomas dropped the heavy statue back to the ground with a loud thud. It felt real.

He looked at the boy. His leg was badly hurt. It was bleeding. Was that a piece of the bone sticking out through his jeans?

"Thank you," the boy said.

"You're bleeding," Thomas answered. "It will get infected with all this dirt in it. It needs to be washed." Thomas picked up the Zippo-lighter again and held it in the air to provide more light.

The boy whimpered. It annoyed Thomas. He couldn't stand children and all their whimpering.

"Wh…where are we?" the boy asked.

Thomas shrugged. "A cave underground, I guess. Listen, I'm looking for a girl. Have you seen her?"

"Nnn…no," the boy said.

"It's very important that I find her."

The boy nodded. "I'm looking for my dog. Buster. I lost him somehow sliding down…"

"We need to find a way out of here," Thomas said. "Fast."

The frustration lingered in Thomas. What if the girl was running around up there somewhere telling everybody what he had done and who he really was? Thomas growled angrily while clenching his fist so hard it hurt. He had to get rid of the girl somehow. He just had to. He had to get back up there.

"What was that?" the boy asked.

"What?"

"I saw something move over there," he said and pointed. "Now it's up there above us. Look!"

Thomas lifted his lighter closer to the ceiling, till it lit up the entire area around them. Human arms and legs stuck out from the dirt everywhere. From both above them and from the sides. The body parts were moving, and when standing still, he could hear muffled screams coming from inside the dirt walls.

Thomas breathed, relieved. Now he knew it was just one of his dreams.

13

Martin Busck had grabbed his wife and child in his arms and run for his life just in time, before the house had disappeared into the ground and buried his beloved brother. Once he felt safe enough further down the street of Blegevej, on the other side of the half-crashed school, he put his loved ones down and stared at the scenery while catching his breath.

It was a true nightmare. No, it was worse. It was horrifying. The entire neighborhood seemed to have fallen into the ground. Martin had a hard time comprehending exactly what had happened. Was this for real? Had entire houses simply vanished?

But that's impossible. Houses don't simply fall into the ground. The ground doesn't just disappear underneath you!

A huge part of the road was gone. Debris was everywhere. In the middle, there was a large hole in the ground the size of three soccer fields. At least. It was huge.

"You think it stopped?" Mathilde asked with a small whimper. "You think we're safe here?"

"I…I," Martin paused. He had no idea what to say to all this. It was so surreal. He had lost his brother, who had been sucked into this enormous thing just a few minutes ago. Mr. Bjerrehus, the man living across the street from him had pulled Martin out just in time, so he wouldn't get swallowed himself, then rushed back to his own house to help his wife. Through the opening that had appeared in Martin's house when David's room disappeared with David in it, Martin had watched Mr. Bjerrehus run across the street. He had watched his every step closely with a wildly beating heart as the man ran, until suddenly the ground caved underneath him when his front foot landed on the asphalt and in the blink of an eye, Mr. Bjerrehus was gone.

That was when Martin decided to run. Run as far away as possible. It had felt like they were running on eggshells, that the ground simply couldn't sustain their weight anymore.

"I'm not sure we're safe anywhere," he moaned.

"I'm scared," Mathilde said.

"Me too."

The ground creaked again, and a blue station wagon that had been dangling on the edge of the hole in the school's parking lot tipped over and fell into the hole with a loud crash. Martin watched it go down. He knew it belonged to Mrs. Krogh, who was a third grade teacher at the school, and who was always first to arrive at the school in the morning and sit in her classroom and wait for the students. She had done that ever since Martin went to the school as a child, and probably still did it. Only, that part of the school where her classroom was, next to the library, wasn't there anymore.

Martin could see his own car on the other side. It had slid down into the side of the hole. Only the back end was sticking out of the dirt. The lights were on and the alarm had set off. Mathilde took a couple of steps further back. In the distance, he could now hear sirens wailing.

He felt his wife's gentle hand on his shoulder. "There wasn't anything you could have done," she whispered.

Martin wasn't so sure. He could think of a lot of things he could have done differently. For once, he could have gone into his brother's room earlier and kicked him out of bed, told him to get up and get some breakfast, go look for a job, go make himself useful. But he hadn't. He had let him sleep in. Given him the time he needed to get back on top. What if he hadn't been such a softy on him? What if he had told him to go take a shower because he was starting to smell in there? Then what would have happened? Would he have been saved? What if he had told Mr. Bjerrehus to stay with them and not go back to look for his wife? He knew. Martin knew he wouldn't make it across the street. Somehow, he had known, but still not told Mr. Bjerrehus. Why? Why was he such a coward?

He stared, paralyzed, at the school building that luckily only had lost the wing with the library and one classroom. All the children had been evacuated to the other end of the school area behind the soccer field. Martin could hear the children whimpering and crying. Or was the crying coming from underneath the ground? Martin was suddenly certain he could hear screams coming from inside the hole. He felt a biting chill run down his spine. Where were all the people? Where had they gone? Where was his brother? Where was Mr. Bjerrehus? The entire neighborhood had vanished into this hole. Houses, fences, entire front yards, cars, people. Were they still alive down there? If they were, how on earth were they supposed to get them out of there again? Digging would take hours, maybe even days.

What the hell were they supposed to do? Just stand there and listen as the screams faded?

14

The boy in my arms was hardly breathing. His pulse was very weak. I felt the desperation as I clawed my fingers into the dirt and desperately tried to dig us out.

I knew it would lead us nowhere. I knew it was impossible, but still I couldn't stop. I had to do something. The intervals between the boy's breaths became longer and longer, and I couldn't stand just sitting there listening to the silence, wondering if each one would be his last breath.

David had a pocketknife that he pulled out and used for digging. He was grunting and groaning next to me, and I got the feeling he was getting all his frustration out by attacking the dirt wall.

Suddenly, as we were digging, the dirt became looser, and I could remove more than before by using my hand. I reached up to scrape off another lump, when suddenly my hand went straight through.

I gasped.

"What?" David asked.

"I think I made a hole in the wall."

I reached my hand inside the hole and waved it. There was definitely air on the other side.

"Really?" David asked.

"Yes! Yes! There is definitely a hole. I've put my arm though it."

"Let's remove some more," David said, and started digging intensively with his small pocketknife.

Minutes later, the dirt surrounding my hand started crumbling and falling to the ground. Air hit my face and my nostrils. Oxygen. David removed the rest of the dirt, while I found my phone and used some of the battery to shine light so we could see.

"It looks like a tunnel," I said.

"It is a tunnel," David said. "It's small, but must lead somewhere."

I took in a couple of deep breaths. It had been hard to breathe properly in the cave with three people sharing the air. It felt so liberating to be able to breathe properly again. The tunnel ahead of us was low and we would have to walk with our heads ducked, but at least we could move. We could go somewhere. At least there was a little ray of hope. The boy in my arms started to breathe more regularly. I felt a deep relief in my heart.

David kicked the last of the dirt wall to make the hole bigger. He felt the ground and the ceiling with his hands.

"Limestone," he said.

"Limestone? We must be really far down then," I said.

"I'm not a geologist, but I know that usually the limestone layers are about four to five hundred meters underneath the surface."

"Five hundred meters underground?" I gulped.

"We're probably not that deep down. In these areas of Jutland, the limestone is closer to the surface. That's why these areas used to be mined. But it is good news."

"Why is it good news?"

"Because it means we've hit the mines. I'm guessing this tunnel is part of what used to be the mines. The world's largest limestone mine, *Monsted kalkgruber,* is very close. It's actually our neighbor. It covers sixty kilometers underground, what they know of, but many tunnels have been naturally shaped leading further away. Caves are shaped naturally by the erosion of the limestone and by water. This area is known for its many underground caves. They probably just didn't know they were building an entire neighborhood on top of them."

"Sixty kilometers. But that's such a huge area. How is that good news? If this is one of the tunnels, then we risk getting lost down here," I lit his face with my phone.

"Because that means there has to be a way out somewhere. We just need to find it. Now, shut off that phone and save the battery for later. We'll feel our way through the tunnel. Follow me."

15

"It's just a dream. We'll wake up in a few minutes and everything will be back to normal, don't worry."

Afrim stared at Thomas like he was mad. Thomas didn't care. He knew a daydream when he saw it. It was just like the time he imagined going into the school with a knife and killing children and teachers. It had been a very vivid dream, but it had been nothing but a dream. Once he snapped out of it, he found himself sitting at his house, staring at the school from his window. There was no blood. No screams. No terror in their eyes.

"It's not a dream," Afrim said. He was still whimpering. Thomas wished he would stop doing that. It was so annoying. He was ruining a perfectly good daydream. Thomas looked at the hands and feet sticking out of the walls and ceiling. Then he laughed. It was one of the better ones. One of the more horrifying ones. But he was getting tired of it now. He blinked his eyes a couple of times to get back to reality. But nothing happened. He was still with the whining boy underground.

Thomas sighed. So, this one insisted on going on, huh?

"Please Mr., we need to help these people. They're stuck," the boy said.

Might as well play along. One of those in there might be your girl.

Thomas Soe used his fingers to dig. Frantically, he dug his fingers into the dirt where the arms and legs were sticking out. Afrim was lying on the ground, holding on to his leg, and crying. Thomas had no idea what he was doing. All he could do was hope that he would find the girl. She had to be in there somewhere...if this was real, and if she was real. He had put the lighter down and managed to dig an entire arm and a leg out, and soon, a face emerged. He pulled the shoulders and got the entire body free from the dirt. It plunged to the ground; a set of eyes behind the dirt looked at him. They belonged to a man. He coughed and threw up dirt. Thomas felt disgusted.

"Damn dirt," the man managed to growl between coughs. "It's freaking everywhere."

Thomas wondered if he should ask him if he had seen the girl, but hesitated. More hands and feet were moving inside the wall, and he started to dig again. A woman emerged from the dirt. Her leg was bent the wrong way. Once she was able to breathe properly, Thomas placed her next to the boy.

Thomas pulled a set of legs, and the body of a man emerged. He was pale and stared at Thomas with empty eyes. Thomas knew that look. He had seen it on Rikke's face when he killed her. He was dead.

"Mr.Thomsen!" the boy yelled when he saw his face. "That's Mr. Thomsen."

It was Mr. Thomsen from number one, Thomas' neighbor who lost his wife to brain cancer last year. Thomas had often imagined killing him. He didn't quite look the way he did in Thomas' other dreams.

Thomas placed the dead body on the ground, and then

returned to the digging. He was hoping the next dead body would be that of the girl. He would like to see what she looked like dead. He continued to dig. It all felt very real. The cold muddy dirt, the people. Thomas was starting to doubt if this was really one of his daydreams. Someone next to him started to help digging. It was the guy that he had pulled out first. He was a big guy. Kind of brusque. The type Thomas got beat up by in high school. His face was bleeding, so was his arm, but he didn't seem to notice. Thomas liked looking at the blood.

He nodded. "Thanks, man." Then he coughed again and spat on the ground. "Name's Brian. Brian Jansen. I believe we're neighbors."

Thomas nodded. He knew who he was. Thomas would lie still at night while listening to the man beat up his wife next door. He would hear her scream for him to *please stop* and *please don't hit me again*. Thomas loved listening to the sound of the man's fist slamming into his wife and her following screams.

"Buster!"

The boy tried to get up to his feet behind them, but couldn't. "I think I see Buster," he yelled" "Over there!"

Thomas turned his head to look. The boy was right. Something was sticking out from the dirt. It looked like a paw. Brian saw it too. "Let's help the kid," he said, and walked to it. He grabbed the paw and pulled it forcefully. Then he stood with the dog dangling upside down.

"Is he…? Is he…?" the boy whimpered.

Brian Jansen shook the dog and made dirt fall off it, then threw it at the boy. "It's dead."

"No!" Afrim screamed. He leaned over the dog and put his ear to his chest. "Please, Buster. Please, be alive."

Afrim went quiet. The woman next to him seemed to be drifting in and out of consciousness. Her leg was bad. The pain had to be excruciating. Thomas couldn't take his eyes off of her. He liked to see people in pain. He didn't know why. It was sick. That much he knew, but he couldn't fight it. Just from watching her, he felt so inspired to write. What great poems he could write about this woman and her pain.

"I can hear his heart," the boy suddenly screamed. "It's beating. His heart is beating. He's not dead! Buster, Buster. You're not dead!"

Thomas and Brian exchanged a look. Thomas found a foot sticking out and grabbed it. "You dig, I pull," Thomas said.

But Brian didn't come to help. Instead, he pulled Thomas' arm. "You know what? Maybe we should rethink this," he said.

16

For the first time in weeks, David hadn't thought about killing himself for even a second. Not since he had looked into his brother's eyes while sliding down, and thought this was it. This was how he would die. It was in those seconds faced with death that he realized he really didn't want to die. He regretted ever having picked up the gun. It was in those seconds after he had woken up inside that strange pocket in the ground surrounded by nothing but dirt and darkness that he had realized he had so much to live for. There was still so much he wanted to do. So many places he wanted to see.

Now he was determined, more than ever, to get out of this place, whatever it was. He was walking through a tunnel of some sort, feeling his way with his hands on the limestone, the woman following him closely with the kid in her arms. He wanted to save them. He wanted to help them and do something good for someone else, for once in his life.

"Do you see anything?" the woman asked, panting behind him. He had asked if he should carry the kid, but she had refused. Something about a promise she had made to herself.

She had told him her name was Rebekka Franck. Once he

heard her name, he realized he knew who she was. She was widely known in his journalist circles. Hell of a reporter who had given up a promising career as a war correspondent to go work for a small newspaper in her hometown. Her decision sent waves of shock through the industry. It was something people talked about. She had chosen it for personal reasons, he remembered people saying. Some people said she was scared. That a bad experience in Iraq had made her quit her job at the prestigious paper. Somehow, David never believed that. There had to be more to her story.

"No. It's all darkness. You sure you can carry the kid? I'll be more than happy to take him for a little while."

"I got it," she said.

"As you will."

David crept further up. He bumped his head on the ceiling. "Ouch." He felt it with his fingers. He was bleeding. He could feel the blood on his fingers.

"You okay?" Rebekka asked.

"Yeah, yeah. Just keep walking and mind your head."

"Luckily, I'm not as tall as you," she said.

David stopped. His hands had bumped into something in front of him. His heart started pounding while he felt it. Panic spread quickly through his body. Whatever it was, it seemed solid.

"What's going on?" Rebekka asked. "Why have we stopped?"

"I…I bumped into something."

"Well, what is it?" she asked.

"It…it seems to be a wall of some sort."

Rebekka became quiet. David kept feeling the wall in front of him. "It's not limestone. It's dirt. I think the tunnel crashed. Maybe when the ground opened."

Rebekka sighed. Her voice was shaking slightly when she spoke. "So, it's a dead end?"

"I'm afraid so."

"Try digging into it with your knife. See how deep it is."

David found his pocketknife and dug it into the wall. "It's deep, Rebekka. It's a wall."

"Walls can be broken. Try some more. There has to be a way to get through. We have to keep trying. It's the only way we have. There has to be a way out. There simply has to be."

17

Buster was getting better. Afrim was so happy to have his friend next to him again, even though he was hurt. A few minutes after being pulled out of the ground, he started moving his legs and ears. It made Afrim's heart jump with joy. Buster had been his best friend for as long as he could remember. Afrim had only been a baby when they got him, his mother used to say. And as soon as he had learned how to walk, Afrim would grab onto Buster's tail and follow him everywhere in the house. Now he touched Buster's broken tail and heard the dog whimper slightly.

"You'll be fine, Buster," he said, and put his head next to the dog's. "Now that we're together, I know we'll be fine."

The woman lying next to Afrim seemed to be more dead than alive. Every now and then she would moan in pain and scare Afrim half to death. It was cold in the small cave, and Afrim missed his parents terribly. Especially his mom. The two men in the cave had started to dig out another arm, but then they had stopped and now they were discussing something. Afrim was wondering if they had realized it belonged to yet another dead body. He pretended not to be, but he was listening in on their conversation.

"I'm just saying it," the big guy Brian Jansen from number five said. "We should think about it."

The tall skinny guy that Afrim knew lived across the street from him, but he hardly ever saw, nodded. Afrim could tell he agreed. Brian lowered his voice, but Afrim could still hear him.

"I tell you, if we keep pulling these people out of that mud, we'll end up getting cramped in here. There simply isn't enough room for all of them. And definitely not enough air. We hardly have enough as it is. We might have to spend many hours down here before they'll manage to dig us out. We need to think about our own survival. In a situation like this, we can't afford to…"

That was when Afrim saw something he had given up hope of ever seeing again. "Mom!"

"What was that?" Brian said.

Afrim pointed and searched for the words. "Mmmm…Mom!"

"What's wrong, kid?" Thomas said. "Did the dog die?"

He looked like he hoped that was the case.

"No…no, look there…over there, it's my mother's fingers sticking out. Look at the ring. It's her ring!"

Brian shook his head. "She's dead, kid. Forget about her."

"No. No. She's moving. I just saw her move a finger. I swear to you. It's her and she's alive."

Thomas looked at Brian. "I'm just saying. There isn't room or air for all of them and us. We have to choose at some point."

Thomas nodded. Brian went to Afrim and kneeled next to him. Afrim growled in pain when he tried to move closer to his mother's fingers. Buster lifted his head.

"Listen, kid," Brian said. "Forget her. Forget you ever saw that finger or that ring. That's my best advice to you."

"No!" Afrim yelled and startled Buster. "You have to save her. You have to dig her out. Please!"

Brian shook his head. Then he slapped Afrim across the face and grabbed his shirt. He pulled his face close to his. "I'm not going to say this again. Your mother is dead, you hear me? She's gone."

"But…?"

Another slap burned across his face. He tried hard to hold back his tears.

"No buts here. It's over. Learn to live with it, kid. Grow up. Or, I swear, I'll kill you as well. Make more room for the rest of us."

Afrim felt the warm tears roll across his face as Brian let go of him. He stared at the three fingers sticking out of the dirt. If only he could. If only he hadn't been hurt, he would dig her out himself.

Afrim felt a hand on his shoulder. It was the lady sitting next to him with the bent leg. "Let it go," she whispered. "Please. They'll kill us."

Afrim became silent. He was biting his lip to hold back the tears, when suddenly he heard something. A new sound. A scraping coming from the wall behind him. It was coming closer. Afrim held his breath.

18

WE CRASHED THROUGH the wall of dirt and landed in a cave of some sort. David and I had frantically dug our way through in desperation, refusing to accept that this could be the end of the road.

Five sets of eyes were looking at us. One of them belonged to a dog. I put the boy in my arms carefully to the ground.

"What the…?" a big guy said, as he turned his head and looked at us.

"Who are you?" the boy with the dog asked.

"I know who you are," the big guy said and pointed at David. "You're my neighbor Martin's brother. You've been staying with him for some weeks now, after that calamity in Syria. I'm Brian Jansen. Where did you guys come from?"

"We were caught in a pocket further down, but dug our way out," I said. "We found a tunnel and followed it here."

The big guy's eyes lit up. "A tunnel, huh? So maybe there is a way out?" He walked closer to us and stuck his head out in the tunnel we had come through.

"You think we can get out that way, Brian?" the tall guy said. I recognized him now as the acclaimed poet Thomas

Soe, who, a couple of years ago, had written some horrifying poems about killing his ex-girlfriend. I never liked the poems much, but the critics did, and the praise was never-ending. He always seemed a little fishy to me...even now.

"We believe we've landed in the limestone mines somehow," David said.

As he spoke, I took a good look around. There was a woman I recognized as the one who had been in the street arguing with another woman when my taxi had stopped right before I was pulled into the ground. She looked bad. Her leg was bent the wrong way and she was in a lot of pain. She wasn't even looking at us. A boy sitting next to her with his dog on his lap had tears in his eyes.

"Is everyone alright in here?" I asked. Something seemed a little off. The boy was sobbing.

"Well, apart from us being stuck hundreds of meters underground, we're all peachy!" the big guy said.

I didn't listen to him. I kneeled next to the boy instead. "Are you hurt?"

"Only my leg," he said.

"What's your name?"

"Afrim. This is Buster." The dog didn't look too well. Still, it wagged its broken tail.

Afrim looked at me like he wanted something from me, like there was a need only I could fulfill. "Please," he whispered.

"Please what?" I asked. "What's going on?"

He was still whispering. "Please help...my mother."

"Your mother? Is that your mother?" I asked and pointed at the woman next to him.

He shook his head. Then he lifted his hand and pointed. I turned and gasped as I spotted three fingers sticking out of the dirt wall.

Oh, my God!

"David!" I said, my voice cracking. "We've got to help her. There's a woman trapped in there!"

I pointed at the fingers. They weren't moving. Immediately, David started digging with his knife and fingers. Soon, we managed to get her arm free.

"It's difficult," David said. "She's stuck pretty far in. If we dig any further, we risk causing the wall to crash."

"Don't do it. You risk killing all of us," Brian said. "If that wall of dirt comes down on us, we're done. She's probably dead anyway. They all are. There's no way they can survive in there, buried in the dirt."

His words made me rise to my feet. I looked around in the dim light from a small Zippolighter placed on the ground and, little by little, I realized she wasn't the only one stuck.

David gasped when he saw it as well.

"We believe they're all dead," Brian said. "We should focus on how we will survive, instead of on rescuing the dead."

My head was spinning. The many body parts stuck in the dirt looked like they'd been taken from some horror movie. I couldn't stop wondering…what if they were alive? How could anyone be so cynical and not at least do something?

"If no one else will, I'll save them all myself," I said, and kneeled next to Afrim's mother's arm and started digging. Seconds later, David kneeled down next to me.

19

It was harder to dig the woman out than I had expected. I was sweating, even though it was very cold underground. David was working hard as well. He was growling while his hands moved agitatedly. I could tell he was as anxious as me. I couldn't bear the thought of leaving this woman in the dirt. I kept thinking of poor Afrim sitting on the ground behind me and the desperation he must have gone through.

It was devastating.

"You're wasting your time and strength," Brian growled. "I say we use our energy on trying to get out of here instead. And you're using up all the air. Our air."

I couldn't believe they could be that cynical. Lucky for us, we had the only knife down here, in case they tried to stop us. I was so happy to have David on my side.

"I think I see her head," David said. "I might be able to grab onto her shoulders if I reach deep inside."

I looked at Afrim. He followed our every move with anxious eyes.

Please let her be alive, please, dear God, don't do this to the boy.

"There's no chance she survived in there," Brian continued

with a sigh. "If you pull her out, you risk all of our lives. All that dirt on top of her will come down on us. I, for one, am waiting in the tunnel."

Brian and Thomas left the cave and went into the tunnel, taking the lighter with them, leaving very little light for us to see. They watched as David reached inside the hole, grabbed onto the woman's shoulders and started pulling. "It's really hard," he moaned. "She's still stuck."

"All that trouble for a dead body. You'll get yourself killed. I'm just saying," Brian yelled.

Afrim whimpered. I could have killed Brian on the spot.

David tried to pull again, some dirt came loose and ended up in a pile next to my feet. My heart started racing. Was Brian right? Would the entire wall come down on us?

"Is she moving at all?" I asked David, and looked inside the hole we had dug.

He shook his head.

"Any sign that she is alive?"

He shook his head again. I took in a deep breath and felt lightheaded. We didn't have much air for all of us.

"Let's both of us try." I reached inside the hole and grabbed the woman's lifeless arm and shoulder.

"On three," David said. "One…two…three!"

We pulled with all of our strength.

It's moving! The body is moving!

Suddenly, it gave in. The body came loose, and so did the dirt surrounding it. A huge pile of dirt crashed on top of us. For a second, I thought I was about to die. I kicked and pushed the dirt away, but it didn't move. Not until David started removing it from the outside and I could breathe again. The body of Afrim's mother was on top of me. I pushed the dirt away and David dragged her out.

"Mom!" Afrim screamed, and tried to drag his body closer to her. Buster followed him closely.

"Oh, great, you made the cave smaller," I heard Brian say. "And for what? A corpse that will start to smell soon?"

"Is she alive?" I asked, ignoring his remarks.

"I…I…" David had turned her around and was looking at her. He wiped dirt away from her face. "She…"

I froze. She didn't look to be alive. Her eyes were closed, she was very pale, and had dirt inside of her mouth.

"We have to clear her breathing passage," I said, and stuck my fingers in her mouth. I dug out all the dirt I could.

"She's not breathing, Rebekka," David said.

"Mom?!" Afrim said, and crept closer. He put his head on her chest. "Talk to me. Say something. Please, Mom. Please, be alive!"

It broke my heart. Thomas and Brian were staring at us. They kept quiet.

"I'm sorry, Afrim. We tried. She's been in there a long time," I said, my voice breaking.

"But I saw her fingers move. I did. I swear it's true. It was right before you came through the wall. I saw her move her middle finger," Afrim said. "She did. She is alive. She has to be!"

The desperation in his eyes was painful. I felt myself tear up. I couldn't bear this. It was just too much.

"I'm sorry, kid," David said. "She's gone."

20

THE SILENCE WAS DEVASTATING. No one wanted to speak. Afrim was crying and crawling on top of his mother's body, pulling himself up on his arms. I looked around and my eyes met Brian's. They had that *told-you-so* look in them. I hated to admit it, but he was right. It was no use. The people had been buried for too long underground. Many of them had probably died while sliding down, getting hit by debris. Others had suffocated from lack of air. Not all had been as lucky as us to land in pockets with air.

"Moms don't die!" Afrim yelled, while punching her chest. "Moms are supposed to be forever, remember?"

I kneeled next to him and put my hand on his shoulder. It hurt like crazy to see the little kid like this, and I kept wondering about Julie, William and Tobias. Did they know what had happened? Did they assume I was dead? Was Julie crying like Afrim, screaming her sadness out while Sune tried to comfort her? I wished there was some way I could tell them I was still alive.

What if you never make it out? Who will take care of her? You're hundreds of meters underground. They'll never be able to dig you out. You'll die from lack of oxygen or thirst.

"Afrim...I..."

"Sh," he said. "I heard something." He pressed his ear closer to his mother's chest. Then he looked at me. "Her heart is beating."

I placed my ear to her chest as well. The boy was right. There was something. A small distant beating.

Could it be? Was this real?

I smiled. "I hear it too!"

Afrim wiped his tears away, then chuckled lightly with relief. "I told you she was alive."

"I think you're right!" I said, startled. I had been so sure she was dead. I couldn't believe this.

David looked like he didn't believe us. He came closer and kneeled next to us. He felt the pulse on her throat. His eyes grew big and wide.

"Oh, my God. You're right. It's weak, but it's there." He laughed. "There's a pulse. I feel it."

We had to move fast now. I began chest compressions. I pushed down in the center of her chest thirty times, then tilted her head back, held her nose and blew in her mouth. I continued over and over until she started coughing. Then, I turned her to the side to let her cough up what was blocking her breathing. Dirt and blood came out of her mouth and was spat onto the ground.

"Mom!" Afrim said. I could hear fear in his voice.

She coughed again, and more blood came out of her. I could tell it frightened Afrim. Finally, she opened her eyes and mumbled something. Afrim crept close to her. "Mom, you're going to be alright. I know you will. They all thought you were dead, but I didn't believe them."

She spoke to him in Albanian. Afrim laughed and hugged her.

"Mom, Mom. Buster is here too," he yelled.

Hearing its name, the dog tried to wag its tail. I could tell it hurt. I looked at David, who was tearing up as well. He was trying to hide it, but his blinking eyes gave him away. Brian and Thomas stared at Afrim's mother, looking baffled and alarmed. I was ecstatic to have proven them wrong. They almost made me lose hope. I wasn't going to make that mistake again. I stared at the wall. My eyes locked with David's. I could tell he thought the same thing as I. If Afrim's mother was alive in there, then who else might be?

21

They started digging again. It made Thomas Soe nervous. He was scared; no that was putting it too mildly…he was terrified that they were going to pull out the girl and save her like they had done the mother. He was hoping she had been killed in the fall. Or maybe that she had been nothing but a mirage. But, if she wasn't, then he hoped she would die in the ground along with all the others.

Soon, they seemed to be pulling out one body after another. Most were dead, but some were still alive. Brian was getting more and more upset and started talking about the two of them getting out of there and finding an escape route.

"This place is going to be filled with injured people, along with dead bodies that'll start to stink in a short while," he said. "We'll all get sick if we don't suffocate from the lack of oxygen first. What do you say the two of us try and find a way out, instead of waiting for death to catch up with us?"

"Where would you go?" Thomas asked, while watching them pull out a body. Thomas stared anxiously until he realized it was a man. He breathed with relief, while Brian babbled on about them leaving. Thomas really didn't want to leave until he was certain they weren't going to find that girl anytime soon. He looked at Brian again and imagined himself licking the blood off of his forehead. Thomas shook his head. He had to try and stay focused.

"I don't know," Brian said. "Anywhere but here. There must be some way out of this hellhole. The way I see it, the two of them came through this tunnel. It's pretty solid. I say we follow it till we find some way out."

"But they came from this direction," Thomas said. "It's a dead end, they told us, remember? Let's stay here."

The woman named Rebekka Franck blew air into the man's mouth. She was in distress. He could tell by the frantic movements. It fascinated Thomas. He liked to watch her. He liked the look in her eyes when she was panicking. The man they had saved started coughing. Rebekka smiled in relief. Thomas lost interest in her. He looked at the handsome man named David Busck. He was pulling another person out by the arm. More of the dirt wall came down and landed on them.

"Oh, great," Brian growled. "They just keep making the cave smaller and putting more people in it. I tell you. They're going to be the death of us!"

Thomas wasn't listening any longer. His heartbeat was drowning out everything else as he watched the handsome man pull out the next body and perform CPR. He felt light-headed. And it was not from the lack of oxygen.

"I say we split. Are you coming?" Brian asked.

Thomas was breathing heavily. He could hardly hear anything anymore. He stared at the girl with the big bruise on her forehead, who the handsome man was trying to revive.

Please be dead. Please don't start breathing. Please be dead.

"If you're not coming, I'll go on my own," Brian said. "I'm not staying here and dying with all these losers. That's for sure."

Thomas held his breath while David pushed on the girl's chest. She didn't move. Thomas felt relieved. Maybe she was dead, after all? David blew air into her mouth. Thomas remembered trying to kiss those lips just a few hours ago, forcing her to kiss him. She had expected him to rape her, but he hadn't. That's not what he wanted from her. He wanted her to show him affection; he wanted her to love him. He wanted her to tell him she loved him. Then he would kill her.

The girl moved. Thomas froze. As he watched the handsome man breathe life into the girl, he kept thinking about how he had enjoyed looking into her fearful eyes. How he wanted it again, how he wished he could hurt Rikke again.

Cheating lying bitch.

When the girl coughed and gasped for air, Thomas knew it was time for him to disappear. None of this felt like a daydream anymore. In his dreams, his victims never survived. They never came back to haunt him. He didn't want to be there when the girl started to tell her story. He turned and looked after Brian who had started to crawl through the tunnel.

"Wait up," he said. "I'm coming. Wait for me."

22

It started to look like a war hospital. Hurt people were lying everywhere in the small cave next to dead bodies. It was a mess. But, nevertheless, we managed to save a lot of people. Afrim's mother had a cellphone in her pocket with a full battery that we used for light, since Thomas and Brian had taken the lighter with them when they left. David and Afrim helped me identify the many bodies. In the dead-pile were a Mr. Frandsen, a Mrs. Krogh and the remains of the taxi-driver I had been in the car with. As I watched his lifeless body with the missing arm, I couldn't help think that if we hadn't stopped…if the two women hadn't been in the accident that blocked the street, then we wouldn't have ended up down here. We would have been long gone.

But I couldn't think like that. It would only drive me crazy.

All I could do was move ahead. Focus on the living and keeping them alive. I was still praying and hoping that they would try to dig us out somehow. There had to be a rescue team up there, trying their best to get us out. All we had to do was wait and hope that we wouldn't run out of oxygen. It was getting tight already, as we were a lot more people to share the sparse air. I was getting tired and sat down next to Afrim and his mother. There were no more body parts sticking out of the dirt. We had done what we could. We had saved a whole bunch of people. Now we were seventeen, I counted, including Brian and Thomas who had left, but would most definitely be back as soon as they realized the tunnel led to nowhere.

Among the rescued was the school's librarian, a guy named Lars who also lived on the street at number thirteen, but had been pulled into the ground just after arriving at work at the school. There was a Mr. Bjerrehus, Afrim's neighbor, he told us. There was a girl who was badly bruised. She told us her name was Malene, but other than that didn't have strength enough to speak and tell us where she was from, since no one in here seemed to recognize her. We had also saved a guy named Michael West, who told us he was simply walking down the street when the ground caved underneath him. He didn't know any of the others in the cave either, he said. I wondered what he was doing in the neighborhood at eight o'clock in the morning if he didn't know anyone. But I didn't ask. I was too exhausted. Besides Michael West, there was Benjamin, a young teenager and his mother Irene, a Kurt Hansen and his wife Annette and, finally, some guy who told us he was an engineer and that he had tried to tell the authorities for years about the possibility that the neighborhood could sink into the ground due to the erosion of the limestone underneath it. But no one would listen. He had been in the neighborhood this morning to drill samples up from the ground to determine the extent of the erosion when the collapse happened. His name was Kenneth Borges. He was a nice guy with chubby cheeks.

David sat next to me and leaned his head backwards. We

stared at the dirt wall in front of us, from where we had pulled out so many bodies. I wondered how many more were still buried further in there.

Big parts of the wall had collapsed and the dirt took up a lot of space in the small cave. I stared into the deep hole that we had dug and wondered how long the big lump hanging free above it would stay in its place. If it came down on us, it would most likely bury most of us. I suddenly wondered if it had all been in vain…digging out all these people just to get them crushed. Most of them were too weak to be able to move or dig themselves out again.

I closed my eyes and tried to picture myself with my family again. How badly I missed them now. How badly I regretted having gone away for the weekend. What if I never saw them again?

"So, what do we do now?" David asked. He was getting weary too. We had used all of our strength digging these people out, and now we were running out of air. I looked into the tunnel and wondered where Brian and Thomas had disappeared to. David and I had come in that way, and I knew it was a dead-end. Why hadn't they come back? Could they have found another way? A way leading out, maybe? They were, after all, mine tunnels. They were connected to something, right? Maybe we had missed something on our way? No, it was impossible. Were they just hiding in the other cave? The one David and I had been in? Just to stay away from us?

"I don't know," I sighed.

There was a lot of coughing and moaning among the rescued people. I had no idea how they were supposed to survive, how I should keep them alive. Or even how I was supposed to stay alive down here.

"I guess we wait and pray that they'll start digging for us soon," I said with a deep exhale. I felt an urging craving thirst sucking me dry from inside. At this point, I would have done anything for a sip of water.

David leaned back his head and closed his eyes. He went silent. I knew why. We didn't have to speak to know what the other was thinking.

There was no way they would make it in time.

23

They had brought in all the heavy machinery, but hadn't started using any of it yet. Instead, engineers were discussing how to approach it. Martin Busck stood behind the police blockage, shoulder to shoulder with his wife and all the other spectators and nervous relatives waiting to hear about their loved ones. He felt so frustrated watching them simply debate and not do anything.

"When will they begin to dig?" he asked his wife. "Why aren't they digging? Can you tell me why?"

"They're probably just being careful. They're afraid that more of the ground will collapse," she said.

"People are down there, for Christ sake. Seconds count right now," he said. "Don't they realize that?"

"I'm sure they do, honey." The baby was fussing in her arms, and she started rocking from side to side.

"I heard they were talking about drilling a hole and sending a robotic camera underground," Ole Sigumfeldt, who was standing on the other side of Martin, said. He lived further down the street from Martin, yet they didn't know each other very well. Ole was a salesman for some electronic company and traveled a lot. Often for weeks at a time, leaving his wife alone with the three boys. Martin often felt sorry for the poor woman, who almost constantly had to struggle with those kids. On top of that, she worked full time for some law firm.

"The site is too unstable right now to use the heavy machinery," Ole continued. "They say the sinkhole keeps growing, so they are waiting. They're taking pictures of the soil using radio waves. They're testing the soil's stability."

"That's just wrong," Martin snarled. "That's going to take forever. They should be digging."

"They will. I just heard them say they'll start drilling holes soon." The man standing next to Ole Sigumfeldt said. Martin knew who he was, but had never really talked to the guy. He knew the family was Muslim, but they had lived in Denmark for many years. Martin had often seen the kid riding his bike around the neighborhood with his Golden Retriever tagging along.

"I'm Sali Berisha, by the way," he said, and reached out his hand. "We live..." Sali paused, then corrected with a thick voice, "We *lived* right next to the school in number four. My wife was in the house when..." Sali paused. "I don't know where my son is. He never made it to school, they told me. The house is completely gone."

"That sucks, man," Martin said. "I'm sorry. I'm waiting for news about my brother. He was sucked down from inside his bedroom."

"I believe my wife and three kids are down there as well," Ole Sigumfeldt said. "The kids never made it to school, their teacher told me. And Karen never made it to work. I just called them...I've been away all weekend on a business trip to Germany. She asked me to stay...for once, to skip a trip and stay home with them. I told her it was a big bonus we would miss out on. She said she didn't care about the money. She was angry with me and didn't answer any of my calls all weekend. I...I never should have gone away."

The three of them went silent while staring down the hole. Martin wasn't ready to lose hope yet. His brother was alive. He just had to be. He didn't get released from ninety days of captivity in Syria just to die in some dirt hole in Denmark. It was simply not possible. It couldn't be.

"Look, they're getting ready to lower someone down the hole," Ole Sigumfeldt said hopefully.

A firefighter wired to the fire truck was slowly going down. Martin watched him anxiously. He'd made it halfway down when the side started sliding. He yelled, and so did the people running the fire truck. As quickly as possible, they managed to pull him back up. The safety zone was then expanded and they all had to move, a policeman told them, while they moved the blockage.

"Get back. Everybody get back; the soil is unstable and we don't want to lose any more people, so please stand back."

"Any news about my brother?" Martin asked, as he was pushed back.

"Any news about my wife and children?" Ole Sigumfeldt asked.

"My wife Blerina and my son Afrim Mustafa are missing," Sali Berisha interrupted them.

The officer shrugged. "I...I honestly don't know what to tell you guys. There is no news about anyone yet. Not that I know of."

"Are you going to try and dig them out?" Martin asked, feeling the anger and frustration surface.

The officer looked at them with a sigh. "Look, guys. I know you're anxious to hear news. I know you want us to move fast, but this situation is extremely dangerous. The hole is still evolving. The soil under this area is eroding, rendering the entire neighborhood unsafe. So, at this time, we're still trying to determine the exact nature of what's going on down there. It could take some time. For this reason, we're being very deliberate, and I understand that being very deliberate is very painful for the relatives. You want us to go in fast. But the only thing that would be more tragic is to send people in and have more loss of life. So, that's the dilemma, and it's a very painful dilemma. We're doing everything we possibly can. Now, if you could start by giving me the names of the people you believe might have fallen into the hole, we'll know who to contact when we have any ne…"

There was a lot of yelling behind the officer, and he turned around to see. Pandemonium had broken out. The dirt sliding down when the firefighter had touched it had revealed something.

"What is it?" Ole Sigumfeldt asked.

"It looks like a car," Sali said.

They moved quickly. The rescuers had seen something. Soon, a crane was lowered down and grabbed the car, pulling it hard and getting it loose.

"It's my wife's," Ole Sigumfeldt exclaimed when it was freed. Big chunks of dirt fell off the Kia as it was carried towards safety.

"It looks like there's someone inside of it," Martin said. Hands were hammering on the windows. He could hear screaming and see a small face.

Ole Sigumfeldt whimpered. "Jacob? It's my kid. I see my kid! It's Jacob! There's another one. I see Christian! Oh, my God, they're alive."

24

We were slowly running out of air. We had gathered all the cellphones from the dead ones and kept them in a pile to use for light, one at a time, until they ran out of battery. After about an hour of waiting, I started panicking. I had been listening for sounds and signs that someone was trying to get down to us, but it was silent as a grave. All I heard now and then was a thud here and there, the sounds of the earth moving. It wasn't done collapsing.

We were buried alive, and if we didn't do anything, we would be dead within a few hours. I was already getting tired and very lightheaded from the lack of oxygen.

"We need to do something," I whispered to David. "We need to find a way out before it's too late."

David nodded. He sat with his eyes closed and head leaned back. He opened them and looked at me. "You're right. But what?"

"Should we maybe go back through the tunnel we came from?" I asked. "I mean, Thomas and Brian left that way and never came back."

"It's too difficult with all these people. Most of them can't stand on their feet, let alone walk through a narrow tunnel where you can't stand upright. It's not realistic. Plus, I don't think they found a way out that way. They would have been back here to tell us if they did. They might be selfish, but they're not cruel. My guess is that they're sitting in the cave you and I ended up in at first and are waiting just like we are."

"What do you suggest?" I asked.

David shrugged. "I don't know."

"Dig," I said. "We could try and dig some more. We managed to break this wall down, maybe there's another one of these walls that will lead to other tunnels in the mine?"

David looked exhausted. I could tell he was having a hard time breathing properly. "I...I'm not sure I have the strength to dig anymore," he said. "I feel so tired. I think I broke a rib falling down. It hurts like crazy when I breathe."

I stared at all the hurt people lying on the ground, the boy Afrim and his mother holding on to each other like there was no tomorrow.

Maybe there isn't.

"I'm not giving up," I mumbled. "I'm not leaving this planet without seeing my kids again."

I grabbed the knife out of David's hand and threw myself at the wall in front of us, where we had pulled all the bodies out. I started digging, pecking with fast and frantic movements till a big block of dirt fell to the ground next to me.

"Be careful," David said. "We don't want the cave to collapse. We don't know how much dirt is on top of us."

I didn't listen. I kept at it. Something felt strange inside my hand. I looked at it. "I think I found something," I said. I grabbed Mrs. Krogh's cellphone and lit up what was in my hand.

"What is it?" David asked.

"Guano."

"What?"

"Bat-droppings. Bat excrement. Cave-dwelling bats. Look. It's like dark brown grains of rice."

"I see it," David said.

I smelled my fingers. "Yes, it's definitely bat poop. Smells horrible." I shone the light on the dirt that had fallen to the ground. There was a whole pile of it. I remember seeing it when I'd just moved into my dad's house. He had bats in the attic that we had removed by professionals. The attic was filled with that stuff. Big piles of it. They told us we were lucky the ceiling didn't cave in from the weight of it.

"So, what do you make of it?" I asked.

David shrugged.

"I'm thinking, where there are bats, there's space to fly, right?"

"You've got a point," David said.

"I have a feeling they can't be far. With this amount of feces, I'd say there's a lot of them."

David rose to his feet. He grabbed one of the cellphones, even though we had agreed to only use one at a time in order to ration our light. He grabbed the knife from my hand and walked slowly around, shining the light on the walls, examining them.

"What are you doing?" I asked.

David stuck the knife into a wall. "Getting us out of here." He'd pecked a few times in the dirt wall when the earth started rumbling again. David gasped and stepped back.

"What's going on now?" I asked, just as the entire wall in front of us came down with a loud crash.

25

MALENE WOKE UP with a gasp. The loud noise terrified her.

Where am I? What was that sound? Oh, my God, the poet. Where is he? Is he still here?

Malene blinked her eyes to better focus. What was this place? A cave of some sort? There were people on the ground lying next to her. She couldn't see their faces in the sparse light.

Oh, my God, he has brought you down here to kill you. This is where he kills his victims and buries them. Oh, my God, you gotta get out of here!

Malene tried to get up, but it hurt. Her back hurt really badly. So did her head. And she was so thirsty. So incredibly thirsty.

She looked in the direction of the light. Two people were standing with cellphones in their hands. They were looking through a big hole in the wall, then at each other. They seemed happy. Who were those people? Why were they happy?

You gotta get out of here, now!

Malene tried to get up once again. Her eyes met those of a

small boy with his dog as she managed to pull herself up through the pain.

Oh, my God. How many people is he keeping down here?

Malene's heart beat fast as she walked past all the people on the ground, carefully trying not to step on any of them. Most looked more dead than alive. Was he simply taking people into this strange place and letting them starve to death? Was that his cruel plan?

Malene felt a chill. It was so cold in here. The boy with the dog looked at her. "Hi," he said.

Malene smiled, but didn't answer. The boy was lying on top of a woman who seemed to be half-dead as well. This was a nightmare. She had to get away from this place and these people. The only ones that seemed to be truly alive were the man and woman with the cellphones in their hands. Malene walked closer to them. They disappeared through the hole.

"Hey, wait for me," she yelled, and dragged her painful body through the hole as well. On the other side, a huge cave opened up.

Malene couldn't believe it. The woman heard her and turned to look.

"You're awake," she said, and approached Malene. Malene froze. Could she trust this woman?

"Hi, I'm Rebekka and this is David," she said.

"Malene."

"Look what just opened up. Isn't it wonderful?" Rebekka asked, and spread out her arms widely.

Malene couldn't quite see what was so wonderful about this place. It was dark and clammy. "Is this the way out?" she asked.

"It just might be," Rebekka answered. "How are you? Are you in pain?"

Malene nodded carefully. "My back and neck hurt."

"You bruised your face as well," Rebekka said.

Malene touched her forehead and remembered hitting the stove and the granite counter in the kitchen. She didn't know if she should tell this woman what happened. She decided to keep it to herself for now. The poet didn't seem to be here.

"A long story," she said. "Where are we?"

"We believe we are in the limestone mines of Monsted Kalkgruber," David said. "We think this is one of the many caves underground that are connected by tunnels."

"The mines? But that's so deep underground? How did we end up here?" Malene asked, but then she remembered. She remembered staring into the deep dark hole while sliding and trying to grab onto something. Then it all went dark.

"The ground caved underneath the entire neighborhood," Rebekka said. "We believe it was a sinkhole. Do you live on Blegevej?"

She shook her head. "I was…visiting someone when it happened."

"Me too," Rebekka said.

She stared at the high ceilings above them. It looked almost like a cathedral when Rebekka shone her lights on it. Underneath the ceiling hung a flock of bats. Malene shuddered. She hated bats, but the air felt a lot fresher in here.

"At least it's better than where we came from," Rebekka said and looked at David. "Let's bring everybody in here." Rebekka looked at Malene. "Maybe you can help?"

26

His fingers had started to bleed. Thomas had been biting them since he and Brian had ended up in an even smaller cave after crawling through the tunnel.

The blood was running down his fingers and landing on the soil, making a puddle that soon turned into a flood.

"Damn it!" Brian yelled. "I can't believe there is no way out of this freaking hell-hole."

The flood disappeared and Thomas looked at Brian sitting next to him. He had blood running out from his ears. Thomas wanted to reach out and touch it, but wasn't sure it was really there. The lack of oxygen made his visions even more vivid.

"You think we should go back?" he asked. He hoped Brian would say no. Thomas didn't want to go back and face that girl. He had hoped it was nothing but a dream, but there she was. With that bruise on her forehead that he had given her when he…when he smashed her into the stove.

Thomas giggled, thinking about it again.

"What the heck are you laughing at, poet-boy?" Brian snarled. "I'm not going back there, no matter what. They're going to die in there, you hear me? All of them. I'm not going down with them. If that's what you want, then go ahead. I don't care. Is that what you want?"

"Nnn…no." Thomas bit his nails again while the flood of blood reappeared. It was soaking his shoes. He moved his feet and it made a splashing sound.

"What the hell is that?" Brian asked.

"What is what?"

"That sound you're making with your feet?"

"I…I don't…know." Thomas felt confused. Was the blood really there?

Brian leaned over and put his hand in the soil. "It's wet," he said. He put his fingers to his mouth and tasted it. "It's water," he said. Then he laughed. "It's water, Thomas!"

"It is?" Thomas felt relieved. For a second there, he had been afraid it was his own blood.

"Haha. Do you know what this means?" Brian asked. He cupped his hands and drank from it. Then he sighed, satisfied.

"No."

"It means we won't die from thirst. Do you know what else it means?" Brian said, agitated.

"No."

"I'm no engineer, but I'm guessing that the water has to have come in here from somewhere, right?"

Thomas shrugged. Brian drank some more water and smeared it on his face, leaving red traces everywhere. Red drops of blood dripped from his chin.

"Have some," Brian said, splashing tiny drops of water on Thomas. "It tastes good."

There was more water now, and it was easy for Thomas to get some inside of his hand. He held it up towards his mouth and looked at it.

"Drink it, you fool. Don't just look at it," Brian grinned.

It didn't look like blood when he had it up close like this.

ELEVEN, TWELVE ... DIG AND DELVE

Thomas closed his eyes and drank. It didn't taste like blood either.

"There you go. See, we feel much better already. Now, I suggest we start digging," Brian said.

"Digging? Where?"

"Where the water came in, you fool. Right there above us. It looks like it's running down from there."

"But what if the ceiling crashes on us?" Thomas asked.

"It might. But it might not. There might be a way out where the water comes in."

"Guess it's worth a try."

Brian dug both his hands into the dirt above them and started digging. Thomas felt indecisive about Brian. Either he was a genius, or he was a damn fool that would end up getting both of them killed.

27

"You take the legs, I'll grab the shoulders," I said to Malene.

She bent down and grabbed the legs, and together we lifted the woman I had seen arguing in the street before the collapse into the air. She had lost consciousness, but was still alive. Malene was strong for a girl her age, I was happy to learn. But she was also in a lot of pain. I could tell by the look in her eyes. Her back was hurting, she had told me earlier. I hoped it wasn't bad. We needed her. We needed as many helping hands as we could get. There were many bats in the cave as we entered it, but few were left after we scared them off, and soon they were gone. I was happy to see that, since I really didn't like bats very much. Still I wondered where they went. If they knew a way out or if they hid in another place.

David took the boy I had carried with me in his arms. We put them all inside the big cave that had opened up to us. I was tired, but so happy to have found it. There was plenty of room for all of us and, most importantly, plenty of air. We were far from out of danger yet, but it was a huge improvement. I was beginning to regain hope that we might be able to survive.

"Let's put her next to the boy," I said.

"It's her son," a voice said.

It was Afrim. David had carried him and his mother in. He seemed to be better. Buster was in his lap. His mother was awake and looking at us. She was still coughing up blood, but seemed a little better. The fresher air made us all feel stronger, I think.

"It is?" I asked with a smile. "This boy?" I pointed at the boy I had carried in my arms through the tunnel.

Afrim nodded. "He goes to my school. His name is Frederic. The woman next to him is Mrs. Sigumfeldt. It's his mother."

My heart dropped. "Really? That's amazing." I felt so happy to be able to bring the two of them together again, even given the circumstances. I thought about my own children again and how badly I wanted to be able to touch them…to hold them in my arms.

"Let's put them real close together," I said. "That way, they'll see each other first thing when they wake up."

"If they wake up," Malene said.

"At least they're together," I said, ignoring her pessimistic remark. I was filled with hope again, and she wasn't going to take that away from me.

"Are there any more?" David asked.

"No, those were the last two," I said.

"So, we're just leaving the dead bodies in there?" Malene asked.

I looked at David. Our eyes locked for a second. I shrugged. "I guess," I said. "We have to think about our own survival now, and getting these people back to the surface. They're already starting to smell. We can't have them in here."

David nodded. "It's the only thing we can do. If…when they dig through to get us, we can tell them where to find the bodies so they can recover them for the relatives. It's all we can do for them at this point."

Afrim's mom coughed. I looked at her and saw more blood coming up. Afrim saw it too. He looked afraid. He held his dog tightly in his arms.

"So, what do we do next?" David asked.

I turned and lit around the limestone cave with my phone. "There seem to be three tunnels leading out of this cave, three other than the one we came from," I said. "I say we gather a search team and try to find a way to the surface. The mines cover more than sixty kilometers of mazelike tunnels. I visited them once many years ago on a trip with my family, but we only traveled through the top layers. We could easily get lost."

"So, who should go?" Malene asked.

I looked around. Mr. Bjerrehus was sitting up. He seemed to be doing better. So was Lars Dalgas, the librarian.

"David and I will go," I said. "You, Lars, and Mr. Bjerrehus here..."

"Just call me Sigurd," Mr. Bjerrehus said.

"Okay. You, Lars, and Sigurd will stay behind and take care of the others. Will you be okay with that?"

Malene seemed skeptical. She was trembling. I didn't know if it was from the cold or fear.

"I promise we'll be back," I said, and put a hand on her arm. "Listen to me. I promise. Alright?"

Malene nodded. "Okay. Just go."

28

It was with some nervousness that David and I left the flock and started walking through the tunnels. We chose one that looked big enough for us to walk through. We had to bend our heads a little, but soon it seemed to open up further and we could walk upright.

The white limestone walls seemed to close in on me at times, and I had to fight the feeling of claustrophobia as I followed David through the first tunnel. Soon, it opened up and we found ourselves in a bigger cave again. David brought out the knife and made a mark on the wall.

"That way, we know which way we came from," he said.

In the cave, I saw more bats hanging from the ceiling. We seemed to disturb them. I shivered when one squealed loudly and flew across the cave, very close to my head.

"What do we do now?" I asked, and shone the cellphone's light onto the white walls. There were four openings leading away. "Which one do we pick?"

David shrugged. "I guess one way is as good as any."

I looked back at the tunnel we had come from, wondering

if we would ever be able to find it again. I had promised Malene we would come back, but it was going to be harder than I first thought.

David picked one, and we continued into the darkness. Every time we came out of a tunnel, he made a mark on the exit, so we would be able to see which ones we had gone through, and hopefully find our way back.

We walked for half an hour or so before we reached a dead end. The tunnel had crashed and was blocked by dirt so we couldn't pass. We turned around and walked back till we reached the cave again. David carved a big X in the side of the tunnel we'd come from, so we wouldn't go through it again. Then we chose another one. It was small and seemed to get narrower as we walked. At some point, I slid and scraped my knee. We walked with our heads bowed until we reached yet another dead-end. More dirt blocked our way.

"Should we try and dig through it?" I asked. "You think there might be a way out on the other side of it?"

David sighed and felt the dirt wall. "It's pretty solid. Probably crashed when the neighborhood went into the ground. It seems like it has crashed everywhere. I just hope it hasn't blocked all the tunnels. Digging will be our last option. We need to save our strength."

My stomach started growling…like a deep groan. I felt the dryness of my mouth every time I moved my tongue. I wasn't sure I would last long without anything to eat or drink.

"Let's take one of the other tunnels," I said, and started backing out of the tunnel. It wasn't big enough for me to turn around. I scraped my knee on the way out again and cursed.

Once back in the cave, I shone my light on the wound. It was deeper than I thought and bleeding a lot.

"Just what I needed," I growled.

"Let's try this one over here," David said, and pointed at an entrance to a tunnel. He had carved a big X on the one we came from as well. Only two were left. If they were blocked too, we'd have to find another cave and another tunnel. I was losing track of the tunnels and caves, and feared that we couldn't find our way back. What if we finally found a way out? Would we be able to go back and find the people? Would I do it even though I'd be risking getting lost in there? I didn't want to think about it.

I followed David into yet another tunnel and we walked for a long time this time. That was a good sign, I thought. We found the end of it, and another cave opened up. David stopped in front of me.

"What's wrong?" I said.

He sighed. "The cave has crashed. It's filled with debris from the collapse. There is no way out."

"Debris?" I walked past David to take a better look. The ground was filled with wood and tiles; I even spotted part of a table and half a couch.

"You think it's the remains of a house that fell into the hole?" I asked.

David went closer and lifted up a piece of broken wood. "Looks like it." He threw the wood further away, picked up a few bricks and moved them. "It's all broken into pieces."

I walked closer and shone the light at the many pieces that used to be a house. I saw part of a chair and a crushed microwave. I walked around, lifting up some things, then uncovering others.

"It looks like the remains from a kitchen," I said. As I spoke the words, I spotted something that brought back the smile to my face.

"Found something!"

"What?" David approached me. I shone the cellphone's light closer to it. An entire pantry was crashed into pieces, leaving at least a dozen cans stuck in the dirt. I pulled one out and dusted the dirt off.

"It's tuna," I said. "And, lucky for us, it's the kind with a pull tab."

29

Afrim was feeling afraid. Not for himself, but for his mother. She was very weak and hardly awake most of the time. When she was, she would smile at him and call him *baby boy* in Albanian.

It was when her eyes rolled back in her head and she drifted off again that he became really afraid. He would lie in the cave with his head on her chest to make sure he could hear her heartbeat. Buster was right next to him, breathing heavily.

"I love you, Buster," he whispered in the darkness.

The old Mr. Bjerrehus was feeling a lot better. He came closer, dragging his hurt leg after him, and sat down next to Afrim. Afrim felt so tired. The thirst was bad. He knew it wasn't good to be this thirsty, or hungry, for that matter. He felt so weak, and fought the urge to doze off. He didn't dare to fall asleep. Who would look after his mother? Who would listen to her heartbeat and make sure it didn't stop?

No, he had to stay awake. Awake and alert.

"Pst, kid?" Mr. Bjerrehus said.

Afrim lifted his head and looked at the old man who used

to live next door. The man who always got so mad at Afrim if he let Buster pee in his hedge. Afrim had always been a little afraid of Mr. Bjerrehus, and especially of his wife.

"I have something for you," Mr. Bjerrehus said.

Afrim was curious, but didn't dare to ask what it was. He merely stared at the man's hand that was in his pocket.

"But, you can't tell anyone else, alright?"

Afrim didn't know what to say.

"Come closer," Mr. Bjerrehus said. He coughed. It was a bad cough. Then, he moaned and leaned his head back with a sigh. "It's okay. Come on over here. I can't reach that far. I hurt my arm in the fall, you see."

Afrim looked at Buster, then at his sleeping mother. Finally, his curiosity got the better of him and he let go of his mother and crawled over to Mr. Bjerrehus. The old man smiled. Afrim could tell he was in pain. Mr. Bjerrehus pulled something out of his pocket and handed it to Afrim. Then he smiled. "Remember. Not a word to anyone."

Mr. Bjerrehus leaned back with a deep moan and closed his eyes. Afrim looked at what he had been handed. It was small bag of bonbons. It was only half full, but there was still a handful left.

Afrim smiled, then looked at Mr. Bjerrehus. "Thank you," he whispered.

Mr. Bjerrehus waved at him without opening his eyes. Afrim reached into the bag and took a bonbon out. He put it in his mouth and sucked on it for a long time. It felt heavenly. Afrim closed his eyes and tasted the sugar, let it melt on his tongue. It felt so good. Then he pulled the bonbon out and put it against his mother's lips. He smeared the sugar on her lips and tried to get it inside onto her tongue. Immediately, she licked her lips, and he could tell she liked it.

"This will make you feel better, Mommy," he said.

His mother groaned for her answer. Afrim could already

feel how the sugar helped him stay awake, how it helped him feel better and less tired. Maybe it would do the same for his Mommy?

He took the bonbon back in his mouth and sucked on it some more before he again put it against his mother's lips. Every now and then, he sent Mr. Bjerrehus a friendly smile, even though the old man didn't notice it, since he was still sitting with his eyes closed. Afrim wanted to thank the old man, but had no idea how. He didn't understand why he had given him the bonbons. Why he hadn't kept them for himself? Afrim thought of all the nice things he would do for Mr. Bjerrehus once they got back to the surface. He most certainly would never let Buster pee on his hedge again.

30

Water was splashing into their faces. Thomas and Brian had made a big hole above them and water was rushing through. It was getting harder for them to dig with all the water running down, but it felt so good. Thomas drank as much as he could from it. It tasted incredible. It had some dirt in it, and a taste of iron and a little oil, but it was water, and he really needed water.

Brian dug a little further, and then stopped. "I think I found the source," he yelled through the water rushing down.

"What?"

"I found where the water is coming from," he yelled. "It's not coming from outside, unfortunately."

"Then where? Where is it coming from?"

Brian crawled closer to Thomas. "It looks like it's a water tank. Probably from one of the houses that fell into the ground. It has a hole in the side where the water is coming from."

Thomas felt disappointed. "So, it's not a way out, then?"

"No. But it's water," Brian said, sounding still very optimistic. Thomas admired him for keeping his hopes up, no

ELEVEN, TWELVE … DIG AND DELVE

matter how bad the situation was. He was a survivor. If anyone was going to make it down here, it was Brian. It was good for Thomas to stick close to this guy. It was the smart thing to do.

Thomas couldn't stop thinking about the girl. Had she spilled the beans on him? Had she told the others how he kept her tied to his bed all night? How he was about to kill her when the ground caved underneath them? Thomas felt so frustrated. He had to get rid of her somehow.

"I think I might be able to stop the water," Brian said. "If we could just find something to put in the hole. It's the size of a fingernail. Do you have any ideas, Thomas?"

Thomas reached into his pockets. He pulled out a pen and a piece of paper. He had once read in an interview with one of his favorite writers that he was always carrying around a pen and paper in case he got an idea for a book and had to write it down fast. Ever since Thomas had read the interview, he had done the same, but he had never used it. The paper was folded several times and wrapped around the pen. Thomas took the cap off the pen and gave it to Brian.

"That's perfect," he said, and crawled back into the hole they had dug. Thomas looked at the dirt ceiling above them, wondering how long it was going to stay up there and stay out of their faces.

Brian disappeared for a second, when suddenly, the water stopped running. A few more drops landed on Thomas's face before it finally stopped.

Brian stuck his head out from the hole. "There. It stopped. Now, we control when and how much. If we ration it, it can last for a long time. It's one of the big ones."

Brian slid back into the cave and put his feet in the mud.

"So, what do we do now?" Thomas asked. He was beginning to feel claustrophobic. He had no idea what time it was. If it was even day or night. He didn't feel very tired anymore.

Not like he had before they had drunk the water. Now he was fresh and awake. But he was still feeling sick to his bones at the thought of them being so far underground. He had never liked being in small places and always avoided airplanes and elevators. He was breathing heavily to try and calm himself down as he felt Brian's hand on his neck. Brian grabbed the Zippo lighter and shut it off. The darkness engulfed them.

"We should save the gas," he said. "You can find your way back without light. There's only one way you can walk. Just feel with your hands."

Thomas froze. What was he saying?

"What do you mean…back?"

"I believe if we keep digging this wall that there's a way out. But we can't do it alone. We need more men. So, you're going back to the others to see if you can get anyone to come here and help us. See if anyone is still alive enough to work. I'll stay here and keep digging," Brian said. "It's the only way out. You tell them we have water; that'll make them come."

"But…You said there was enough for the two of us. Are you going to give it to them? Don't you think we'll run out pretty fast?"

Brian laughed. "Nothing in this life is free, my friend. Let's just say that now we have the upper hand, shall we? Tell them anyone who works for me will get water. But only if they work. Now go!"

31

THERE WAS MURMURING between several of the people in the cave. Malene had no idea what was going on. She had been sitting at the entrance ever since Rebekka and David left, wondering if she would ever see them again. The earth still sighed and moaned like it wasn't done collapsing, and every now and then she could hear a loud thud, the sound of dirt falling and maybe blocking their way back.

Maybe blocking our way out.

Several of the hurt people had woken up since they left. Now they were discussing the situation amongst themselves, some panicking and yelling at each other, while others tried to shush them and tell them to not panic. They had no light except for that from the cellphones. Everyone wanted one, but they had only handed out two to save batteries.

"Sh? Did you hear that?" Lars, the school librarian, said. "I think I hear drilling. I think I hear something!"

They all went quiet for a few seconds. Even Malene tried to listen. But she couldn't hear anything.

"You're crazy," Michael West said.

"No, I'm not. I heard it. I'm certain. Listen," Lars continued.

"It's all in your head. We're never getting out of here," Michael West said.

"You don't think they're trying to get us out?" Mrs. Sigumfeldt said. She had been the last to wake up. Her scream had filled the cave as she realized her unconscious son was right next to her. Then she had screamed again and again while looking at her leg that bent the wrong way, until the old guy, Sigurd Bjerrehus had managed to calm her down.

"Your son is breathing. He's only unconscious, as were you until a few seconds ago. He'll be fine. He's alive," he had told her. "We'll get help. Somehow. Some way. The important part is to not panic."

Mr. Bjerrehus had been repeating that sentence over and over again as more people woke up, realized the severity of their situation, and felt the thirst and hunger they all suffered.

Malene's watch was still working. The glass was broken, but it still showed time when she pressed the little button on the side of it and the display was lit up. They had been down there all day. It was almost seven o'clock, and none of them had eaten since that morning. Malene hadn't eaten since yesterday evening, before she was picked up by Thomas Soe. It was getting late and it had been hours since Rebekka and David left on their rescue expedition. Malene was starting to wonder if they'd ever see them again. Would they get lost? Would they return if they found a way out? Would they abandon them? She thought about what she would do. She was no hero. That much she knew. There was no way she would go back if she found a way out. What if more of the ground came down? What if the tunnels were suddenly blocked after you had gone all the way back. And for what? A couple of hurt people with broken arms and legs that could hardly move? They were never going to make it. There was no way they could walk through the tunnels, even if they could get out that way.

They promised. She promised to come back. She'll be here soon.

Michael West turned to look at Mrs. Sigumfeldt. "You wanna know what I think? I think they believe we're all dead. There's no way anyone could survive that. That's what they think. They're not drilling or digging to find us. They have the area evacuated. They have a police blockage surrounding it. But there is no way they'll risk their lives trying to dig us out."

He might as well have hit Mrs. Sigumfeldt in the stomach. She gasped for air and leaned forward in panic. Sigurd put his arm around her shoulder. Then he spoke to Michael West.

"There's no need for that," he said. "There's no need to be talking like that. You're scaring everybody. Especially the kids."

"Well, I'm just telling the truth here," Michael West continued. "Someone has to say it the way it is. The only way for us to get out of here is if we walk through those tunnels over there on our own."

He got up to his feet and wiped dust and dirt from his pants. "Luckily for me, I'm able to walk," he said. "I'm leaving."

"Michael," Mrs. Sigumfeldt said. "Don't leave us down here. Take me with you."

"You're in no shape to walk," he said. "I can't carry you. Sorry."

"Michael, Goddammit. Please?"

"I'm sorry. I can't carry you and the kid. I can't."

"Michael! You can't just leave us." Mrs. Sigumfeldt was crying now. Not that she cared much, but to Malene it sounded almost like he was breaking her heart.

But then again, Malene didn't know any of these people and, to be frank, she didn't care much about them either.

No one said anything more as Michael West started walking towards one of the tunnels. Malene watched him closely as he disappeared through the hole. Back in the cave, Malene heard Mrs. Sigumfeldt whimpering and crying. Without anyone noticing, Malene had stolen one of the cellphones from the pile. It had belonged to one of the dead ones back in the first cave. They had made the pile of all their cellphones from everybody's pockets to save them for later and save the batteries. Everyone had been instructed to only use one at a time, but Malene didn't trust any of these people. She had wanted to be able to light her way if she ever got stuck in one of those tunnels by herself. If she had to run.

Malene felt the phone in her pocket, while looking at the pathetic bunch of people lying and sitting in the limestone cave. There was no way any of them were going to survive. Michael West was right about that. He was the smart one for leaving.

Malene sat for a few minutes more, debating with herself, before she decided to get up and follow him.

32

We found more stuff. Good things. Besides the cans of tuna, we found a box of Danish Butter cookies, a few were still whole, the rest mostly crumbs, but still edible. I found a candle that I put in the pocket of my jacket. I found a box of oats and some wrapped crackers. Best of all, I found three bottles of water. That was going to keep us going for a little while longer. Thirst was the biggest threat to our survival at this point.

"Let's grab as much we can carry and get it back to the cave," David said.

I felt a sadness and slight desperation as we left the cave and started going back. Somehow, it felt really scary to have to walk back down there again. I had liked the feeling of going somewhere…of getting away from that cave. I was imagining that we got closer to the top as we walked through the tunnels, and kept hoping for a way to the surface with every turn we took, every time we reached the end of a tunnel. Now we had to go back. David felt the same way, I could tell. He walked slowly, yet he was determined.

"Now I only hope we can find the right tunnels," he said.

The pressure felt heavy. Here we had food enough for the people to be able to at least make it through the rest of the day and night. How horrible it would be if we got lost...if they starved to death while we tried to find the right way back.

I wondered if David was thinking the same thing. I felt bad for being selfish and wanting to continue to find a way out, and decided to keep it to myself.

David stopped in a cave. I lit the entrances to the tunnels, and we found the one with only one mark, and then continued. Suddenly, the earth rumbled and dirt fell down from the ceiling.

"Get back, hurry," I said, and pulled him out of the tunnel, right before it crashed in front of us.

He landed on top of me, and then rolled away. "That was close," he said. "Thanks."

"No problem." I tried to get up, but I had hurt my head in the fall and I felt dizzy. David saw it.

"Are you alright?" he asked.

"I will be," I said. "Just give me a second."

David sighed. "Now what do we do?" he asked. "The tunnel back is blocked.

I sat up; the dizziness was almost gone. My head was still hurting like crazy. David lit the other entrances with the cellphone. "We could try this one," he said. "We haven't been through it before, but with a little luck, it'll lead to the same cave."

"It's a long shot," I said.

"I know," he said, and sat down next to me. I felt tears pricking my eyes. "Let's take a little break first. Maybe we could eat something?"

I looked at the food. I had taken off my jacket and gathered it all inside of it, shaping a vagabond-bundle.

"It was supposed to be for the people that are trapped

down there," I said. "I don't know if it's right for us to eat from it."

"I haven't eaten since yesterday. I need something to keep me going," David said. "Or I'll never make it down there."

"It just feels wrong," I said. I felt the hunger as well, but probably not as bad as he did, since I had a big breakfast at Lone's house before I left. I reached in and handed him some crackers. He ate them greedily. I grabbed a couple as well. The guilt was eating at me, but so was the hunger.

"You want one of these awful wrapped cakes?" I asked.

He grabbed one and ate it. I tried it as well. It wasn't as bad as it looked. Then I opened a can of tuna. We ate with our fingers. David even drank the water it had been in.

We rested for a few minutes. I put my head on his shoulder and we sat leaned against the limestone walls and closed our eyes.

Another rumble woke us up. A loud thud reminded us where we were and that the earth was still collapsing around us.

It was truly terrifying. But there was something worse. Another sound. A scream that pierced through our bones.

33

"Did you hear that?"

I looked at David. He nodded. "That didn't sound good."

"We have to get back to them," I said, and got to my feet. "Something is wrong."

More screams followed. Terrifying screams. My heart pounded. I wondered about the children…Afrim and Frederic. They were the ones I worried most about down here. They were so young and fragile. Both of them had their mothers who were badly hurt. A terrifying thought hit me.

What if one of the mothers had died?

"We have to find our way back somehow," I repeated.

"All we can do is try one of the tunnels and see where it leads us," David said, and got up as well. "I'll mark the ones we've been through, and hopefully we'll find the right one at some point."

The prospect of running into these tunnels, not knowing where we would end up, terrified me, but not as much as the thought of what might have happened to one of the boys. The screams did sound an awful lot like they came from a child.

"Let's do it," I said.

ELEVEN, TWELVE … DIG AND DELVE

"Okay," David said, as he exhaled. "Guess we'll take the one closest to the one we were supposed to go through before it crashed."

"I'm right behind you."

I grabbed my vagabond-bundle. The screams were still echoing through the mines, making me fear what we would find once we got back there, *if* we ever got back there.

I walked behind David for what felt like forever. It seemed to me that the screams were getting closer. At least that gave me some sense of security…that we were, in fact, going in the right direction.

And we were. The tunnel opened up, and suddenly we could walk upright. David started to run, and I followed as fast as I could, while still holding on tightly to the bundle of food. A thousand images ran through my mind. I was almost certain it had to be Afrim who was screaming. I prepared myself for it. I told myself that he probably lost his mother and needed to be comforted right now. I thought of the possibility that it might have been his dog, and at some point hoped that was it. It would be devastating for the boy to lose his friend, yes, but at least he would still have his mother. Afrim's mother had been in terrible condition when we left. She had been very pale and hardly awake at all. I feared for her life most of all the people in the cave.

Please don't let it be her, dear God. We're so close with the water and food now. Just a few more minutes and we'll have what she needs. It will help her, God. I know it will. Please don't let her die a few minutes before we arrive.

"I think we're getting closer," David said. "I think we took the right way."

We were running as fast as we could. The screams were more of a whimper or a loud cry now. It sounded more like someone scared than someone sad. It gave me hope that it might not be Afrim.

Maybe something happened to Frederic? Maybe his mom woke up and found him dead? Oh, God, did Frederic die? He was awfully weak!

The tunnel took a turn and we kept following it, when suddenly, David stopped. The tunnel had ended in a new cave. From there, there were two tunnels we could take besides than the one we came from. David lit his cell phone to see if there was a mark on any of them.

"There," I yelled. "There's a mark over there! We've been here before."

David led the way through the next tunnel, and even though they all looked so alike, I was certain I remembered being in this one before. Halfway through it, the crying got louder, and we knew we were very close. David stopped suddenly and lit his cellphone. In the light, we saw Malene. She was standing in the tunnel, her back leaning up against the limestone wall with a terrified look on her blood-smeared face. Her eyes were fixated on something on the ground. In her hand, she was holding a cellphone.

David shone his light on the ground.

It was a body. Michael West's dead body was lying in a pool of blood. His face and chest were full of holes.

34

Martin Busck stood next to Ole Sigumfeldt while they watched the giant crane set the car on the ground and let go of it. Ole whimpered when he saw small hands knocking on the windows.

"I'm going in," he said, and jumped the police blockage.

Martin watched as some officer tried to stop Ole from getting closer, but then let him go, once he realized it was his family that was in the car.

Ole ran around the edges of the hole and Martin's heart pounded hard while watching him slip and slide down at one point, then pull himself up by a tree and get back on the unstable ground and keep running.

Martin put an arm around Mathilde and the baby, knowing he would have done the same for them.

Ole gesticulated and yelled at the firefighters and officers once he reached the car, and they let him open the door. Martin heard the boys scream.

"Daaaad!"

He pulled them out and hugged them, while crying heavily. Then he stopped. "Where are the others?" he asked. He looked at Jacob, the oldest, for answers. Jacob shook his head and cried.

"Where is Frederic? Where is Mom?"

Ole looked at the officers for answers. "Where is my wife? Tine? Frederic? Where are they?"

The officer next to him shook his head with a shrug. "We don't know."

"They fell in the hole, Dad," Christian said, crying. He hadn't let go of his father since he opened the door.

Jacob was crying and holding onto his father's arm, leaning into his chest. "They…they just disappeared. One minute they were in the street because there had been an accident…then the next, they were gone, Dad. They vanished into the ground. I screamed, then tried to get them, but the car started moving as well. Then we fell. The car slid and spun around. Everything went dark inside the car. I tried to start it once it was still again. I tried to start it, so we could honk the horn, but it only worked for a little while, and I don't think anyone could hear us. We were buried in that dirt, Daddy. It was so scary. We were really afraid."

Ole hugged his son and kissed him again and again, then kissed Christian before he kissed Jacob again. Ole was crying, his body shaking.

Then there was a loud rumble. The earth shook for a little while, some of the edges of the hole started sliding again, and Martin took a step backwards. There was someone behind him, but he moved fast as well. The children started screaming again. An officer approached Ole. "We need to get you to safety. The hole is still evolving. It's not safe here."

"But…But…my wife, my other kid?"

"We're doing the best we can, sir. Please, just get behind the blockage again. We'll let you all know when there is news to tell. But you must…you must prepare yourself. It's not good. They've been down there for many hours now. It is safe to say that not many can have survived this, if any at all."

A loud sob rang through the crowd of spectators. One woman bent over and started crying. Martin looked at Mathilde, and their eyes met. Boy, it had been close. They almost lost everything. He tried to do as the officer had told them to. He tried to prepare himself for the fact that he might never see his brother again. His baby brother that he had adored ever since the day their mom brought him back from the hospital. His baby brother, who had always gotten himself into trouble, and whom he had helped out so many times he would never be able to pay him back.

Martin tried hard to imagine him being dead down there underground, but somehow, it didn't work. There was something inside of him that said it was impossible. With all he had gone through, it was almost like his brother was immortal. Like a cork in the water, he always had a way of floating to the top.

Martin hugged his wife and held her tight.

"He's gone, Martin," she said. "You have to let him go."

Martin drew in a deep breath. He knew his wife was right. He just couldn't. He wasn't ready to give up on him. Not yet.

35

"Malene? Are you alright?"

I walked around the corpse and grabbed her hand. She gasped and looked at me like she hadn't noticed us until now.

"He…He was…he wanted to find a way out. I followed him. I heard noises in the tunnel in front of us and thought it was him, but when I got here, I found him like this. He was lying on the ground. I…there was no light. I stepped on him and fell. I…I fell right on top of him, on his bloody face."

"That explains the blood," David said. "Let's get her back to the others. Did you walk far before you found him?"

She shook her head, whimpering. "A few minutes maybe."

"Okay. We're almost back then," David said.

"What do you think happened to him?" I asked, looking at the many wounds in his face and chest. They seemed deep.

David kneeled next to the body and shone his light in the wounds. They were pretty nasty. "Looks like he was stabbed. It doesn't look like a knife, though. The holes are more round, but deep."

Malene shivered.

"Did you see anything before you stepped on the body?" I asked. "There had to have been someone else in the tunnel."

"I…I didn't," she said. "I was trying to get to the other end of the tunnel. I was saving the battery of the cellphone to make it last longer in case I got lost down here, so I was walking in the dark, feeling my way through the tunnel. Then I stepped on him and fell. I didn't see anyone or anything. But, like I said, I did hear strange noises."

"What kind of noises?" David asked.

"I…I don't know. Just noises. Maybe a thud and some splashing, feet running, I don't know. But whomever did this had to have come through the other end where you guys came from. Didn't you see anything?"

David and I looked at each other. I shook my head. "No. All we could hear was you screaming."

"Let's get back to the others," David said. "Maybe they know something. I don't feel like we're safe in here."

Malene sobbed. I put my arm around her and gave her a hug. She was shaking. Her hands were bloody. David started walking.

"What about the body?" I asked.

"Let's bring it back to the other dead ones and keep them together," David said. He picked up Michael West and carried him on his shoulder. "We need to tell everyone what happened anyway."

We walked in silence through the tunnel and ended up in the large cave. The first to meet us was Sigurd Bjerrehus. "What happened?" he asked. "Who was screaming? Oh, my God, what happened to you?" he asked Malene.

"Michael West was killed inside the tunnel. Malene found the body," I told him, and helped her sit down while David carried the body of Michael West into the smaller cave where we had left the others who were dead. I pulled out one bottle of water and gave it to Afrim to give some to his mother.

"Small sips. Just a little bit at a time. Moisten her lips with it, try to make her drink. You share this bottle with your mother."

Afrim gave me a beautiful smile. I heard grumbling and murmuring behind me.

"Why are they getting water and we aren't?"

I turned and looked to see Lars Dalgas and Mrs. Sigumfeldt. They looked angry. "Anyone who has a problem, come to me," I said. "The woman is hurt very badly. The boy needs hydration as well."

Lars Dalgas growled something I didn't hear. He looked at the bottle of water like he would pull it out of the boy's hands. Afrim was holding it close to his body.

"Touch the boy, and I'll make sure you never touch anything else again," David said. He had taken out his knife and was showing it, so there was no doubt in anyone's mind that he was serious.

"How?" Sigurd asked. "How was he killed? Did the tunnel crash on him or something? I heard a loud thud just before…"

I shook my head. I spoke with a low voice. I wasn't sure we should scare everyone further. Especially not the children. "He was killed. Stabbed to death. Did anyone besides Malene and Michael West leave the place while we were gone?"

Sigurd Bjerrehus looked baffled. "I…I mean…several of us have been up to pee, finding some privacy in the tunnels."

"Who?" I asked. "Who went out to pee?"

"You two were gone for quite a long time, so basically most of us. I know I did. Lars did. Even Mrs. Sigumfeldt. I helped her get to her feet. She held onto my shoulder as I helped her into the tunnel, then I left her till she called for me. Afrim was also out at one point. I helped him as well. Besides that, many of us have been walking around…walking inside the tunnels just to have a moment alone and to stretch our legs. The hours are long in here; the wait, a chilling affair, when you don't know if you'll get out of here ever again."

"What about Thomas and Brian? Have you heard anything from them?" I asked. "Have they come back?"

Just as I spoke the words, I spotted Thomas Soe coming out of the same tunnel we had found the body in. He was smiling.

"Hi, everyone. So good to see you're all still alive."

I heard a small cry behind me and turned to look at Malene. She crouched and looked like she was trying to hide herself, while staring at the approaching Thomas.

36

He had found a new tunnel. While walking through the first tunnel, the only one he knew of, he had suddenly found another opening, leading to another tunnel. He figured it had opened up after the earth shook again, and more of the ground collapsed. Somehow, the wall had broken down and revealed another tunnel for him to take. His first thought was that it would lead out of here, so that he could find his way out and never have to deal with Brian or see the girl again.

But, he wasn't that lucky. No, instead, it had lead right into this huge cave where everybody else was. At least he thought it had. Somewhere in between where he left Brian and his arrival in the cave, he had blacked out. He had no idea if he had walked in the same tunnel; he believed he might have been walking through several of them, but he wasn't sure. He also thought he had been walking in a pool of blood in one of the tunnels, but was certain it had been all in his imagination, as was the blood on his shoes.

It's all in your head, Thomas. You know it is.

As he walked closer to the flock, he spotted the girl. She

was sitting on the floor squirming and twisting her body, looking like she was about to scream if he came any closer.

He felt the pen in his pocket, and wondered if he should stab her right away. Just walk up to her and stab her. But, what good would that do him? She'd be dead, yes, but he'd still be stuck down here and everyone would be really mad at him, maybe even kill him for what he had done.

It wasn't a good solution.

He thought of what Brian had said, and decided to go with his plan. Even though all of the people in front of him looked like stabbed corpses, he spoke to them like they weren't. He was getting better at ignoring all those small reality-slips.

"We found water," he said.

"Thomas?" Rebekka Franck asked.

"Yes. It's true. Brian and I found water."

"Thomas, what is that on your shoes? Is that blood?" she asked.

The girl whimpered again. Thomas, all of a sudden, remembered the sound from when she had been in his house, tied to the bed. He looked at her and saw blood running from her forehead into her face. He imagined himself using the axe, dividing her face into two pieces. He imagined the sound of her skull cracking.

Like the sound of a watermelon falling to the ground being divided into a thousand pieces.

He remembered it well from when he had done it to Rikke. He remembered the sound so vividly.

"Thomas, do you have blood on your shoes?" the annoying Rebekka asked.

Thomas looked down. Yes, he had blood on them, but he had been soaking in blood, hadn't he?

"Where did it come from?" Rebekka asked.

Thomas could feel how the tension was tightened in the

cave. Everybody who was awake was staring at him, waiting for his answer.

"Brian says anyone who comes back with me and helps to dig will be allowed to drink from the water," Thomas said.

"Thomas, did you kill Michael West?" the handsome David asked.

Thomas opened his mouth to speak, but couldn't get a word out. He had no idea what to say. The fact was, he might have. He didn't remember.

"So, who wants to go back with me and get water?" he asked. "Brian told me he thinks he can find a way out, but we need many hands to dig. Everyone willing to work for him will get water."

Rebekka Franck stared angrily at Thomas. She took a few steps towards him. All eyes were on him now.

"So, you're saying that not everyone will get some of that water, is that it? Only those willing to work?"

Thomas nodded. "Yes. Those were his words."

"So, what about the people almost dying here? Those that are hurt and sick from thirst. They're not able to work and dig. Shouldn't we help them first? Make sure they survive?" Rebekka asked.

Thomas took a step backwards. The small skinny woman scared him a little. He pictured himself grabbing her neck and snapping it. Like a match you could break with just a finger. It would be that easy. She was small. So why did he fear her? Why did she frighten him?

Thomas wanted to run away. It was getting dangerous for him here. He took another step backwards, but walked right into David who grabbed his arm. "You're not going anywhere, buddy. You're staying here with us."

37

WE DECIDED TO tell everybody what had happened to Michael West. I wasn't sure it was a good idea to scare people further, but they saw David carry him away. They knew something was wrong, and the incident with Thomas made them start questioning what was going on.

We gathered everyone in the cave and David put Thomas on the ground, while keeping an eye on him.

"Michael West was killed inside of one of the tunnels," I said.

Murmurs spread in the flock. Almost all of them were awake now. The only one still drifting in and out of consciousness was Afrim's mother. She didn't seem any better at all. She was heavily dehydrated and needed water. She had lost a lot of blood.

Mrs. Sigumfeldt looked at me. "Killed? But…but…what on earth do you mean?" She looked like she was about to cry, but restrained herself.

"He was stabbed to death. We found him in his own blood in the tunnel we came through," I said.

Mrs. Sigumfeldt gasped and put a hand over her mouth. "Oh, my God."

"We believe Thomas Soe did it. He came through the tunnel, had blood on his shoes, and didn't deny it when we asked him."

"What do you have to say for yourself?" David said.

Thomas Soe looked baffled. It was like he was trying to speak, but couldn't. "I…I don't know what to say."

"That's not an answer," Mrs. Sigumfeldt yelled. She got up on her feet. I was impressed with her agility all of a sudden. Maybe the adrenalin caused it. She was awfully interested in this Michael West's death. As far as I knew, Michael West had been nothing but a stranger to the neighborhood. A bypasser at the wrong place at the worst possible time.

"Did you kill him?" she asked.

"I…I swear, I…I don't know," Thomas said.

What kind of a weird answer is that? Either you kill someone or you don't. Is he playing us?

"What do you mean you don't know?" I asked. "Are you denying it?"

"Yes." He looked up at me. He seemed confused. "I didn't do it, okay? All your sudden questions took me off-guard. Of course I didn't kill the guy. It's ridiculous."

"How did you get blood on your shoes, then?" Sigurd Bjerrehus asked. He too was on his feet, looking agitated.

Lars, the school librarian, stood up as well. "Leave the poor guy alone. He probably got blood on his shoes by walking through the tunnel, just like Rebekka and David. Or are we to assume that you killed him too?" He pointed at my shoes. I looked down and noticed they were soaked in blood, as were the bottom part of my pants.

"You two came through the same tunnel with blood on you. David is even the only one of us who has a knife. Why are we not accusing any of you?" Lars continued.

He did make a fair point. The rest of the group seemed to think so as well. They looked at us accusingly.

"How do we know you're not just trying to cover up by blaming someone else?" Mrs. Sigumfeldt said.

I looked at David. "They're right," I said. "We don't know if he did it. As a matter of fact, it might be any of us in here, right? I mean, who hasn't left the cave to pee or to get a few seconds of privacy?"

Everyone looked at each other, then back at me.

"If Thomas Soe didn't kill Michael West, then who did?" Sigurd Bjerrehus asked.

I inhaled and looked at David again. He shrugged.

"I'm not waiting here to find out or to become the next victim," Lars said, and walked over to Thomas. He reached down and grabbed his hand, then pulled Thomas up. "You said you found water. Lead me to it, and I'll work for you. I'll dig till my hands bleed if it means I get to drink all the water I want. At least I'll be doing something. I do not intend to stay here and wait for starvation or one of my neighbors to kill me."

On that note, Lars and Thomas left us. I looked at the rest of our group. "Anyone else who wants to go, you're free to do so now," I said.

No one did. "Okay. So here's the situation. We have some food, not much. About twelve cans of tuna, a box of oats, a packet of crackers, some broken cookies, and a little water. If we're smart about it, we can survive on it for a long time. The important thing is to remain positive. Don't lose hope. I know they will be looking for us. I know they're digging for us right now. We just have to be very patient. But the fact remains that even if we're super-optimistic about things, the best you can say is we're in deep shit. The only thing we can do is to be strong, super-disciplined, and united. We have to stick together through this, and help each other out the best we can."

On those words, I handed out the water and food, rationing it so there would be enough for several days. It was getting late. The first day in the mines had almost passed and I had a feeling it wasn't the last. As people dozed off after having eaten small rations of tuna mixed with water and crackers, I looked at what was left. Almost all the water was gone already. Rationing it further would keep us alive for a few days, maybe. But no more than that.

II

DAY 4, OCTOBER 9TH 2014

SURVIVAL OF THE FITTEST

38

I was so unbearably thirsty. So hungry it literally hurt. The emptiness in my stomach felt like a fist pushing downward. It was painful. I had given most of the water to the sick people, thinking I could better manage with no more than a few sips a day. By noon the fourth day under the surface, we had run completely out of water, even though I had rationed it well. I was so hungry I had even considered trying to catch a bat and eat it, even though I knew they could carry all kinds of diseases. We hadn't seen any of them in a very long time.

There was a great sense of powerlessness among us. We didn't know if we were being rescued or what was going on on the surface because we didn't hear any noises from machines or anything. We had tried to find a way out through the tunnels, but hadn't succeeded, and as the hours and days passed, we became too weak to try anymore. We were even too lethargic to get on each other's nerves. No one bothered to fight. Every now and then, someone went into a panic, but it was getting more and more rare. We simply didn't have the strength.

Prayer helped us get through the day. We had started a

prayer group for those who wanted it. Most of us did. It became the highlight of the day. It was a good way to get some of the anger and frustration out. It started on the second day when Afrim had fallen to his knees and cried out, "God, please help my mother! Please save her!"

Compelled to show compassion, David and I had kneeled as well. Afrim's mother started mumbling in Albanian, lying pale and weak on her back. We joined in. It didn't matter that we had different gods. Soon, others joined in, and little by little we started having prayer sessions every day at noon before I served the day's only meal. It became a daily ritual for everyone. People of different faiths, on their knees, in repentance and desperation, praying and whispering. Some were crying. I know I was from time to time, thinking about my family. Others were mystified, as if they couldn't quite believe they were on their knees, begging God to rescue them. A God they, until a few days ago, weren't sure they believed in.

On the fourth day, right before prayer and lunchtime, David was sitting next to me. He was feeling weary. I could tell by looking at him. He kept closing his eyes and leaning his head back. No one wondered about Michael West or what happened to him anymore. At least no one spoke about it. We were way too focused on merely surviving. We hardly went into the tunnels anymore. Since no one had eaten or drank much for days, it wasn't like nature called us to step out. We stayed close together; everyone was instructed to never leave the cave and go into the tunnels alone, even though I couldn't help wondering if the killer could still be among us.

Sometimes, we could hear the ground rumbling and thuds from dirt falling to the ground inside the mines. The smell from the corpses nearby was getting bad. So was the smell from all of our bodies in the cave...our fetid unwashed bodies. It was constantly cold in the cave, the temperature remained about eight degrees Celsius (46 degrees Fahrenheit) all night and day, Kenneth, the engineer, told us. With no food in my stomach, I soon started to shiver with the cold. David put his arm around me and tried to warm me. I felt like I could hardly move. My legs were hurting, so was my stomach, and I couldn't stand the feeling of thirst. I was amazed at how fast the body reacted to these dire conditions…how fast I became affected by it.

"We have to do something," I said to David. "We'll die from dehydration. We need to get some water somehow."

We hadn't seen or heard anything from Brian, Thomas or Lars for several days, neither had we heard anything from the surface, except for those sounds people now and then imagined hearing.

"Did you hear that?" they would say.

I would always nod and smile and assure them it was most certainly the rescue team working to get us out of here, then tell them to just be a little more patient. I felt it was my job to keep up their spirits in a place where hopelessness and anger otherwise ruled.

It was getting harder and harder to stay positive. I missed my children like crazy and refused to accept never seeing them again. I kept going through my last conversation with Sune in my mind over and over again. We hadn't left off on good terms. He had been annoyed with Julie, and that bothered me. Every now and then, I would sob and wish I had told him I loved him, or had even been able to say goodbye to the kids. Did they know how much I loved them? Had I told them enough?

"What do you suggest?" I asked. The fatigue overpowered me again, and I had to close my eyes. It was the dehydration doing this to me. I knew it was, but I couldn't help it. I tried to fight it, but all I wanted to do was to sleep. Sleep and dream that I was back with my loved ones, hugging and holding them in my arms and never letting go.

"We could try and go back to where we found the food. See if there's more. Maybe if we look again, remove some more debris, rocks and planks, something will show up," David said. He had brought this up before, but every time we had tried to find our way back, we had ended up getting lost in the tunnels.

"It's too hard," I moaned. "I'm so tired. I need to rest. How will you even find your way back there? It was pure luck that we found it in the first place. We risk dying even trying," I said. "We're too weak now."

"What about Brian and the water Thomas said he had found?"

I opened my eyes and looked at David. I had thought about it too. Several times. But going back there and telling him we wanted water was a really bad idea. He would only give us water if we worked, he had said. If we dug. That would mean a lot of the others couldn't get any. David and I could, yes. Sigurd Bjerrehus too. But the rest? They were badly hurt. I didn't believe that Brian would let us get enough water to give to them as well.

"I don't think he'll let us have it voluntarily," I said. "But maybe if we put a little pressure on him."

"What are you thinking?" David asked.

I looked at the remains of the food. There were still several cans of tuna, cookies and crackers. If we rationed it further and only ate one spoonful of tuna mixed with water each day, it could last for a long time. We didn't need the food as much as we needed the water. It was all down to survival now. We could go for longer without food. We needed water desperately.

"No," David said. "We'll starve if we give them our food. There's barely enough as it is."

"We'll just offer them some of it. Not all. We keep a few cans for ourselves, then ration it, maybe only eat every other day. We need the water more. And my guess is they haven't eaten at all since we fell down here. They must be pretty desperate by now. I think they'd be ready to make a deal."

David sighed deeply. "I'm not fond of doing any kind of business with those guys…I really don't trust them. I know people like them."

"It's our last chance," I said. "They said they have water. We need it. There's no other way out, the way I see it."

David nodded. "Alright then. You've convinced me. We'll do it."

"I'll gather some food," I said, and got up. My legs felt so weak I wondered if they could even carry me through the tunnel.

David pulled out the knife from his pocket and looked at it. "But if they try anything, I swear, I'm gonna kill them all."

39

"Look who comes crawling!"

Brian had a weak look to his face. All three of them did. Their cheeks had fallen in and their eyes were glaring feverishly. Brian lit his lighter as we came closer to better see us.

David and I approached them, holding a cellphone in front of us. It only had a little battery left. All three of them were sitting on the ground of the small cave, dirt on their faces and clothes. Above them, they had managed to dig a big hole.

"Come to join the winning team, have we?" Brian said.

I shook my head and sat on my knees. I put three cans of tuna on the ground, along with three wrapped up cakes, the rest of the cookies, and half of what was left of the crackers. I had kept the oats at the cave, since they kept us feeling full longer than any of the other food, even if we only ate a handful every day.

All three looked desperately at the food. "You have food?" Brian said.

"We want to make a trade," David said. He was flashing his knife to make sure they knew we were able to defend ourselves in case they tried to steal the food. "You get this, we get water."

"And you light this," I said, and pulled out the candle I had taken on the first day and hidden in my pocket until now.

Brian shook his head. Thomas stared at us. He had that look in his eyes that frightened me slightly. It was creepy. It was like he was there, and he was looking at me, but wasn't really. Like someone daydreaming, only he was smiling blissfully. I was wondering if he was well. Maybe the starvation had made him hallucinate. I had heard about that happening before. He had that madman look about him. I didn't trust him. Someone who could write so vividly about molesting and killing someone else had to be sick in their mind, in my opinion.

"No," Brian said. "Definitely not. I'm not sharing the water unless you come work for me. We've dug a large tunnel up through the dirt. But it's going too slowly. We need more hands."

"But you're weak from hunger," David said. "You need food to keep working. We can give you that."

Lars kept staring at the food on the ground. He looked like he was ready to kill Brian to get to it. "Give them the water," he said. "We need the food, Brian. My stomach is growling so loud it sounds like the ground is rumbling."

"That's the sounds caused by the layers of muscle in your intestines squeezing food that isn't there," David said. "I went through a long period of starvation when I was kidnapped in Syria. My doctor explained this to me later…that the sound was a gurgling set off by the stomach trying to digest what's not there, made louder by the echo chamber of an empty stomach. Each contraction will cause you to think about food even more. Do you know what happens to a body when it starves? Most of us are familiar with the unease of going too long without eating. That's because, after just a few hours without food, your body has burned through most of its supply of glycogen, the most easily reachable source of energy stored in your body. After two or three days without food, most people will have used up their entire store of glycogen. In these first few days, symptoms are mild, including hunger pangs, bad breath, headaches, and a feeling of exhaustion. While hunger pangs—the strong contractions of the stomach I talked of earlier—generally pass within these first couple days, it's after seventy-two hours that a real hunger is in effect. In the days that follow, the body begins to break down stores of energy in fat and muscle, essentially cannibalizing itself to survive. As your bodies harvest any available energy stores to power the brain, the body rapidly sheds both muscle and fat, and levels of important nutrients like phosphorous and magnesium are depleted."

David paused and saw the effect his little speech had on them. They looked terrified. I was amazed. He was quite the speaker.

"I think you should take the deal, Brian," David continued. "You won't last long without food."

"And we're thirsty," I said.

Brian kept staring at the food. I could tell how much he wanted to attack it. Then, he nodded. "Okay. I'll let you fill your bottles."

"Twice," I said. "We come back when they're empty and fill them once again. We're a lot of people, remember?"

"And you light her candle," David continued.

Brian bit his cheek, while considering the proposal. He wasn't pleased with our demands, but I could tell he was desperate. His eyes were wide, his insides screaming for nutrition.

"Alright. You win."

40

"I can't stand it anymore!"

Afrim lifted his head to look at Mr. Bjerrehus, who had started yelling. His eyes were flickering.

"Keep calm, Sigurd," Mrs. Sigumfeldt said.

"I can't," he said. "I can't keep calm anymore. What are we waiting for? Starvation or thirst to kill us? I can't just sit here and wait for death!"

"Rebekka and David went to get water from the others," Mrs. Sigumfeldt said. "You'll feel better as soon as you get something to drink."

Afrim had seen people in the cave panic from time to time. Even Mr. Bjerrehus, who usually kept his cool, who usually was the one calming everyone else down. But he had never seen a look in any of their eyes quite like the one Mr. Bjerrehus had in his at this moment.

It scared him. Afrim liked Mr. Bjerrehus. He liked him a lot. He had been the one to give him the bonbons when they had nothing to eat. Afrim still had two of them left in his pocket. He was certain they had saved his mother's life. She was getting better. At least that's what Afrim told himself. She was still coughing up blood on the floor and wheezing badly when she breathed, reminding him of Wheezy in Toy Story. But when she was awake, the few times a day, she would look at him and smile. She would call him baby boy in Albanian and hold his hand. Those were the moments he felt so happy. They were worth the wait.

Buster seemed to not be doing too well with the lack of water. He had lost a lot of weight and was whimpering constantly. His leg was getting better, and on the third day, he had run around in the cave, searching for water and even barking at the bats. But now he was hardly moving at all anymore. Afrim petted his head, while wondering how long the dog could survive without water.

"I have to get out of here," Mr. Bjerrehus yelled. "I have to get out. There has to be a way. There simply has to be."

"But there is no way out!" Mrs. Sigumfeldt cried. She was holding her son in her arms. Frederic stared at Mr. Bjerrehus with wide eyes. Afrim had talked to him a few times since he woke up, but he didn't seem to want to talk much. Afrim knew why. He was simply scared to death. As was Afrim. But he had to stay alert; he had to watch over his mom and Buster. He didn't have time to be scared about anything other than losing those he loved.

Where are you, Daddy? Are you coming for us? Are you searching, digging for us? Or have you given up by now? Please, Daddy. Mommy's sick!

"We've tried everything, Sigurd," Mrs. Sigumfeldt said. "Please sit down and be quiet. You're scaring the kids."

"I…" Mr. Bjerrehus was spinning…around and around like Afrim's top used to do when he played with it in the driveway.

He looked crazy, Afrim thought, and he had seen his share of crazy people when his aunt was admitted to a mental institution and Afrim had to go visit once a month.

Mr. Bjerrehus' eyes looked like theirs. They were sad, and

he looked like a scared little boy too. Afrim knew about being scared. When his aunt had stayed with them after she came to Denmark from Albania, he had been very scared of her. Sometimes, she had screamed all night long. She had tried to attack Afrim's dad with a knife in the kitchen. Afrim's mom had told him she wasn't well…that many years ago she had to flee from Albania in the trunk of a car with her husband, and that he was shot. She was forced by soldiers to shoot her own husband. Then the bad soldiers did some *bad things* to her. Things that made her *lose her mind*. Afrim knew what it meant to *lose your mind*. It was what his aunt and all those people at the mental hospital had done. And it was what Mr. Bjerrehus was about to do now.

41

We filled the empty bottles from the water tank and gave the food to Brian. He lit my candle and I carried it back, careful to keep it lit. Back in the cave, they all looked perplexed when we walked in.

"What's going on?" I asked.

Afrim had been crying. For a second, I thought something bad had happened to his mother or dog, but they were both the same as when we left.

"It's..." Afrim tried hard to act grown up, but that made him seem even younger than he was.

"Sigurd left," Mrs. Sigumfeldt said. "He got up and started babbling about not being able to take it anymore, then he left."

"Didn't you try and stop him?" David asked, while I walked around, letting everyone take small sips of the water.

"If he wants to run out there and get lost, then it's his problem," Mrs. Sigumfeldt said. "I have enough on my plate."

"I thought we agreed to stick together and not let anyone go anywhere alone," David said.

Several of the others started murmuring. I could tell they were angry, and it made me frustrated. I decided to skip prayer time and go directly to lunch. Maybe getting something to fill the gap in their stomachs would help calm everyone down. I looked at the guy named Benjamin who hadn't been involved much in anything. He was a teenager, eighteen or so. He had kept mostly to himself, sitting in the corner with his mom, Irene. David had told me they were neighbors to David's brother Martin, and that he had seen him around, especially at nighttime when the boy went out with his friends. He didn't know anything else about him, and neither the boy nor his mother had wanted to share about themselves or participate in any debates with the rest of us.

"Benjamin. Could you help me serve lunch?" I asked. "Now that Mr. Bjerrehus isn't here anymore, I could use an extra hand."

Benjamin got up. I opened a can of tuna and grabbed one of the empty cans. I divided the tuna into the two cans and poured water on it to make it last longer.

"We need to ration the food further now that I had to trade some of it for the water," I said. "But I believe we'll manage somehow."

Mrs. Sigumfeldt moaned angrily. "I can't stand more tuna in water! I'm so hungry!"

"We all are, Tine," I said.

I asked Benjamin to get the crackers and hand them out along with the handful of oats. Meanwhile, I fed everyone with tuna. With Mr. Bjerrehus gone, we were still twelve mouths to feed. I approached Afrim. I gave a spoonful to his mother, who was capable of lifting her head to eat it.

"Thank you," she wheezed feebly.

I looked at Afrim. "Your turn," I said.

"What about Buster?" he asked.

I sighed and put the spoon back in the bowl.

"The dog isn't eating our food," Mrs. Sigumfeldt said. "I'm

sorry, sweetie, but we all need to survive here. There is no way we're feeding the dog."

Two others murmured in the back. "I'm with the lady," the man named Kurt yelled. "You're not feeding the dog with our food or our water."

"Please," Afrim pleaded. "He hasn't had any food or anything to drink for days. He'll die."

My heart pounded. I felt bad for the boy. It was terrible.

Suddenly, Benjamin spoke up. "Let him have something to eat like the rest of us," he said. "It's the kid's best friend. He's a family member. Haven't you ever had a dog?"

I looked surprised at the young guy who had hardly spoken a word all the time we had spent down there.

"No way," yelled Kurt back. He got up to his feet. He was a big guy. "If you give any food or water to the dog…then… I'll…" He lifted his fist in anger.

David came up behind me. He had his hand on the knife. He was about the same size as Kurt. "You'll what?" David asked.

Kurt grumbled, then spotted the knife in David's hand and backed down. He murmured some more.

"Give the dog my portion," Benjamin said.

"No, Benjamin," his mother, Irene, said.

"Yes. This is what I want. Give him the water and the food I was supposed to have. I can wait another day."

42

AFTER EATING, THERE really wasn't much else to do besides take a nap. It had become the routine for all of us in the cave and it was, in fact, Malene's favorite time of day. Dozing off with food in your stomach, even if it was just a little bit, was the best part of the day…today more than any other day, since there had been so many murmurs and complaints among people in the cave. Malene hadn't taken part in the discussion, nor had she uttered her opinion about the boy and his dog, whether it should be allowed to drink the water and eat the food or not. She knew she felt sorry for the boy, and she didn't want the dog to die, but she didn't want people to get angry with her as well, so she kept it to herself. Mainly because she was a coward and didn't dare to speak up. It had made her so happy when Benjamin spoke up. She had looked at him admiringly, and she did that again now that she put her head down in the dirt. Right before she closed her eyes, she glanced in Benjamin's direction and her eyes met his. Then she smiled. He smiled back, right before he closed his eyes. Malene closed hers as well, and soon she dozed off.

She had a nightmare. She was dreaming about the night

she had spent in Thomas Soe's room while he was staring at the blank screen. Malene was tossing and turning, groaning in her sleep, crying for help, trying to run, but he grabbed her leg and hit her again and again.

Malene woke with a gasp, just in time to look into the eyes of Thomas Soe. He put a piece of dirty clothing on her mouth and signaled her to be quiet. Malene felt like she was choking. She had the taste of dirt in her mouth again, just like when she had been inside the ground.

Malene tried to scream. Thomas slapped her across the face. She whimpered and fought to get loose. Thomas held her tightly.

"Sh, my pretty girl," he whispered, close to her ear. "Don't make a sound. Or I'll break your neck. It's up to you."

He lifted her up from the ground. Malene looked desperately at the others in the cave, hoping and praying that someone would see or hear her.

Help me. Someone, please help me!

Thomas shushed her again, then giggled, and carried her out of the cave. Malene tried to kick and scream, but no one heard anything, and Thomas was way too strong for her.

He carried her through one of the tunnels, the one where she had followed that Michael West guy and later found him dead.

Had Thomas killed him? *Of course he had*, she thought to herself. He was a sick monster. She regretted not speaking up about him when she had first seen him, or when they had accused him. She should have said something. Why didn't she?

Because she was afraid. How she loathed herself for being such a coward. She had wanted so badly to speak up when they had asked him if he had killed Michael West, when they had asked him about the blood on his shoes, but as she had opened her mouth to speak, he had sent her a look. Her eyes had met his, and in his smile, she could tell she would be next if she didn't keep quiet. She knew he would kill her if she spoke up. Malene thought it was smart of her to not say anything. She thought that was what kept her alive, kept him from coming after her.

But she was wrong. He had come, after all, and now he had taken her away from the others. Where was he taking her? Back to the other men?

He put her over his shoulder as he hurried through the tunnels. They ended in a cave, before he stormed into another tunnel, which ended in yet another cave. Malene cried and wondered if he even knew where he was going, or if he was just running till they got lost? But, somehow, it seemed like he knew exactly what he was doing. He seemed like he knew exactly where he was taking her. He had a light, it seemed. Was it a flashlight? She couldn't tell from where she was hanging, but she thought it was.

How did he get ahold of a flashlight? How did he find his way through the tunnels and caves so easily?

Malene cried hard, thinking this had to be the end of everything for her. She had cheated death a lot of times in the last few days. It was, after all, only cats that had nine lives.

4 3

He had seen him in the bar of the hotel every night since the collapse, but never talked to him until this night after dinner. The skinny guy with the green Mohawk, leather band with spikes around his neck, and black make-up on his eyes had stood out in the crowd from day one. He had showed up on the first day, around three hours after the sinkhole had swallowed the neighborhood. He had a couple of kids with him, Martin had noticed. He seemed like a nice guy, despite his appearance, which Martin didn't care much for.

"Do you mind if I sit?" Martin asked, and pulled out a barstool.

The guy shrugged. "Suit yourself."

Behind the bartender, the TV showed pictures of the site with the text rolling underneath stating: *Day 4 after the collapse. Doctor's say survivors are no longer a possibility.*

There was no sound on the TV, and Martin was glad there wasn't. After yet another entire day of waiting behind the police blockage for news about his brother, the last thing Martin needed was another journalist trying to tell him there was no longer hope of finding anyone alive.

They had accommodated all of the relatives and those who had lost their homes in a local hotel in downtown Viborg. Who paid for it, Martin didn't know. Probably the county. He didn't care. All he thought about was his poor brother.

"So, I take it you have relatives who disappeared in the collapse as well?" Martin asked.

The guy had a beer in front of him. He had hardly been drinking it. He kept picking up a beer nut between his fingers and letting it drop to the counter again, then repeating the motion, again and again.

He nodded. "My girlfriend."

"Ouch. That sucks," Martin said. "I'm Martin, by the way." He reached out his hand.

The guy took it. Martin had noticed he was missing two fingers on his right hand.

"Sune."

"I have a brother who sunk into the ground. I tried to save him, but couldn't. I swear, I could still hear him hollering for me, even when I couldn't see him anymore. The sound haunts me at night. I've barely slept since it happened."

"Me either."

"How many children do you have?" Martin asked.

"Three. Only one with Rebekka. She has a daughter from a previous marriage, and I have a son. They all miss her. I have no idea how they're supposed to go on living without her."

"Do you think she might still be alive?" Martin glanced at the text on the TV screen once again. He hated how they just blurted it out, like it meant nothing to them. In the beginning, he had watched all the shows, all the experts, and listened to what they had to say, but by now he knew it only spread more fear in his heart. They didn't know any better than he did. They just speculated. Any fool could do that.

"I know it's impossible. They tell me it is, but…" Sune paused and looked up at the TV screen as well. "I just feel in my heart that she's still alive. It's hard to explain. Maybe I'm just not ready to let go yet."

Silence broke out between them. Martin ordered a beer. He thought about telling Sune that he felt the same way, but hesitated. He drank the beer while watching TV. They had been digging for four days now. At first, they had drilled a hole and lowered a camera, but they saw nothing but debris from houses and cars. With big cranes, they had started removing the dirt, while firefighters tried to dig out carefully with their hands whatever showed when dirt was removed. It took forever, and Martin found the wait to be devastating.

"So, what do you think is worse," he asked Sune, "waiting at the site while they dig, or the nights when you wait for them to start again, thinking, wondering if this night is the time when your loved one will take their last breath?"

Sune exhaled, then drank from his beer. "All of it," he said.

"I keep fearing that they'll hurt someone with the crane when they let it dig into the dirt. I hate when they lower that thing into the ground."

Up until now, it had mostly been cars and bricks they had dug out. But there had been a body too. The man steering the crane hadn't seen it and dug the claw into the dirt, then pulled out a leg. The spectators had all screamed. The firefighters managed to save the remains of the body of Mrs. Frandsen from number ten, but the terror in the spectators' eyes couldn't be removed. It was burned into their memories, and every time the claw was lowered into the ground, they feared it would be someone they knew this time.

"I can't help thinking there should be another way, you know?" Martin said.

For the first time since Martin sat down next to him, Sune looked directly at him. "I know," he said. "There really should be."

44

"Where is Malene?"

I had just woken up. David was still half asleep when I shook his shoulder. The rest of the people in the cave were all awake. It was Benjamin who told me they couldn't find Malene, that she was gone when he opened his eyes. He was standing in front of me looking upset. I woke up David.

"They can't find Malene," I said, once his weary eyes looked back at me.

"What do you mean they can't find her?" he asked.

"I've looked everywhere," Benjamin said. "She was here when we went to sleep after our meal. I looked in the tunnels and called her name, but she wasn't there either."

"What about Mr. Bjerrehus?" I asked. "Has he come back?"

I had saved his meal for him, thinking he would be back later, once he realized running off didn't get him anywhere.

Benjamin shook his head. "No. He's gone too."

"They've probably just run off, thinking they'll find a way out," Kenneth said. "Probably got themselves lost."

"Better for us," Kurt said. "Less mouths to feed, if you know what I mean."

I overheard his comment. I didn't care much for it. "Should we form a search team to go find them?" I asked David.

"If they want to run into those tunnels and get lost and die from thirst and hunger, I say we let them," Mrs. Sigumfeldt said. "I'm with Kurt on this. The less mouths to feed the better."

"We can't just leave them to die, "Benjamin's mother, Irene, said. "What if they hurt themselves somehow or got stuck. Wouldn't you want us to look for you if it was you?"

Kurt grumbled, then backed down. "I'm just saying it increases our chances of surviving. If you want to go out there and get lost as well, be my guest."

"I'm staying here," Mrs. Sigumfeldt said. "It's no use anyway. I can only focus on me and my boy now."

I looked at David. He shrugged. "I say we go look for them…it's the least we can do."

Benjamin nodded. "Yeah. What's wrong with you people anyway? They're your neighbors and you can't even help them?"

"I don't even know the girl," Mrs. Sigumfeldt said. "Do any of you?"

"Mr. Bjerrehus has been your neighbor for many years," Irene said. "We all know him."

"But none of us ever liked him," Kurt said. His wife Annette pulled on his arm. "Stop saying things like that, Kurt."

"Why, when it's the truth?" he said. "I didn't like the guy. Why should I risk my life for someone I really didn't care about? There, I said it. It's just the way I feel."

"Just because of that old thing…" Annette mumbled.

"Well, it was a big deal for me," Kurt snapped at her.

Annette shook her head. "Sigurd and Kurt weren't exactly the best of friends," she said, trying to justify her husband. "Let's just leave it at that."

"Why?" Kurt exclaimed. "Why should we leave it at that? Why shouldn't we tell it the way it is?"

"Kurt…don't. Stop it."

"I'm tired of pretending it never happened," he continued. "Why not tell everyone how you and him…how you and he…"

"It's been so many years, Kurt. Don't start…"

"I'll damn well start whatever I feel like. I'm sick of pretending like it never happened, like you never…like you and him never slept with each other on the night of the Christmas Banquet. Everybody saw you, Annette. Everybody watched you and him as you were at it on the dance floor. Do you have any idea how humiliating it was for me? No, I haven't spoken about it. No one has, but everybody knew it. Everybody looked at your growing stomach in the months after, wondering if the child even belonged to me, or if it belonged to him."

Annette turned her head away. "It's been twenty years, Kurt. We were drunk. You know it didn't mean anything. Will you never let it go?"

"No, dammit. I won't. I have pretended for years that it didn't happen, that we're all past it. I've pretended like he's my son, like I don't constantly wonder if Mark is really mine. But I'm constantly dragging this horse around, all these questions; I can't keep it in the past, Annette. I can't. Is he even mine?"

Kurt was standing up now and yelling at his wife. "Is he, Annette? Is he my son? Answer me!"

Annette didn't say anything. Her pause was painful.

"That's what I thought. You know what? I've had it. I've had it with you, with this entire neighborhood and all its secrets."

Kurt took one last look at all of us, then stormed into one of the tunnels. I looked after him, wondering if we would ever see him again.

45

Thomas stroked the girl on the cheek while humming a lullaby his mother used to sing to him as a child. Just like he used to do to Rikke when she was asleep. The girl was whimpering in her sleep, tossing and turning.

"Hush, my little baby," he whispered. "Everything is going to be alright. I'll take care of you."

She had fought him for hours while he held her down. It wasn't until she calmed completely down and fell asleep that he let go of her.

"I'm gonna take such good care of you, Rikke," he whispered, and held her in his arms while rocking her back and forth. "This time, I'm gonna do it right. It's for your own good. I can't have you telling on me to all the neighbors, can I? What will they think of me? I can't have that. So, now you stay with me, you hear?"

Thomas had found a cave that no one else had been in. He wasn't much of a sleeper, so every time the two others fell asleep, he roamed the tunnels and explored every one of the ones nearby. He had mapped it all down on his paper that was supposed to be for good ideas, and now he found his way around easily. Back when that David guy, the handsome one, and that small skinny journalist-girl had found the remains of a house in the tunnel, Thomas had been watching them. He had followed them through the tunnels, and after they had ripped the area for food and what else they could find, Thomas had gone through everything as well. He had found lots more food that he had kept to himself and eaten, then he had found a flashlight that he didn't tell anyone about, and some other stuff, like a butcher's knife. Afterwards, he had walked through the tunnels, destroying every mark that David had made, making new ones so they wouldn't find their way back again. He wanted to keep the place to himself. And, so far, he had succeeded. Now he had the girl too, so everything was complete.

He felt complete. And he wasn't going to go back to the others…to Brian and Lars. He didn't need them anymore. He had found a barrel in the remains from the house, and every day, he had stolen water from Brian's tank, filling up bottles from the house and carrying them to his secret place. Now the barrel was full, and Brian's tank was close to empty. It wouldn't be long before he found out, and Thomas wasn't going to be there when he did. He wanted to be here with his beloved, and never ever let go of her again.

"As long as you're here with me, Rikke, I won't feel so alone. Boy, how I've missed you. I missed you so much it HURT! Do you have any idea how bad I have hurt, Rikke, huh?"

Thomas took in a deep breath and hugged the sleeping girl. He saw blood on her face and wiped it off. More blood ran across her face, and Thomas felt anxiety. Had he killed her? Had he killed her and didn't know it? Thomas blinked his eyes a few times and the blood disappeared. He felt relieved. He really wanted to do it differently this time. He didn't want to happen what had happened to Rikke. He had lost it, blackened out, and when he got back to being himself, it was too late. She was gone.

He put himself on top of the girl, pressing her down, while crying and thinking about how much he loved Rikke.

"Why?" he cried. "Why did you have to leave me?"

The girl moaned and moved underneath him. Thomas crept closer to her face and caressed her gently.

"It's just you and me now, baby. No one will ever come between us again. No one, Rikke. No other guy. I'll forgive you for what you did to me. I have to. Then we'll spend eternity in here together. Just the two of us. Forever and ever."

Thomas sniffled, then grabbed the chains he had found in the remains of the house as well. He looked at them and laughed. Whoever used to live in that house must have had a kinky basement. There were leather ankle cuffs connected by a heavy shackle. While strapping one end of it on the girl and the other to his own ankle, Thomas thought about his neighbors and tried to picture who among them would engage in sex games using these. He couldn't imagine any of his quiet and decent neighbors being into bondage, but it turned him on simply thinking about it.

Thomas closed the straps and lifted his ankle, which was now attached to the girls'. He was at least twice her size, so if she wanted to go anywhere from now on, he would have to agree. He watched her calm breath, thinking how much better everything was now that they had each other. The girl moaned and moved. She was going to wake up soon. She would be hungry once she woke up.

He'd better start preparing his welcome-home dinner.

46

MALENE FELT SORE. Her body was hurting badly when she woke up. Where was she? She blinked her eyes several times to see better. Then she gasped. Suddenly, she remembered everything. The guy, the poet, had taken her away from the others. She had tried to fight him, she had kicked and tried to scream, but he had kept her in the cave, held her down till she ran out of strength. He had been caressing her hair and cheek while calling her Rikke. Who was this Rikke, and why did he call her that?

Oh, my God! He's going to kill me!

He didn't seem to notice she was awake. What was he doing over there anyway? Malene stretched her neck to see better. He was working on something and whistling. What the hell was he up to now, the crazy bastard?

Think quickly, Malene. This is your chance to get away. He's not watching you. He's busy doing something else. Run!

If only she could get into one of the tunnels. She could hide in there till he gave up looking for her.

What is he doing over there? What's on the floor?

Malene couldn't see much, since he was the one holding

the flashlight. His body cast a grim shadow on the wall of the cave. Malene tried to move, to slide carefully across the ground, thinking he might not notice her if she stayed close to the ground. It was when she tried to move that she saw it.

What the hell has he put on my leg?

It was a chain. It was heavy, and as she moved, it made a sound. Thomas didn't seem to notice. She looked at the chain that continued into the darkness. Where did it end? What had he chained her to? She had to get closer. Malene tried to slide further across the ground, hoping the chain wouldn't make another noise.

Thomas was singing loudly, like he was enjoying himself and what it was he was up to.

Chop chop, Sweet Charlotte
Chop chop, till he's dead
Chop chop, Sweet Charlotte
Chop off his hand and head.

WHAT WAS HE SINGING? It sounded like that old song from that old movie Malene's dad used to show her. The one with Bette Davis.

Hush...Hush, Sweet Charlotte.

Only the lyrics were different. Like a ghoulish version. It gave her the chills. Malene took in a deep breath and tried to follow the chain to see where it ended. But as she did, she finally got close enough to see what Thomas was up to. In front of him on the ground lay Mr. Bjerrehus. Or what was left of him. He was being chopped into pieces, the meat of his stomach and leg being cut off by a butcher's knife in Thomas' hand, while he sang his little song. Malene felt nauseated. She gagged, and a few seconds later, she threw up.

Thomas heard her and stopped singing. He turned his

head and looked at her. "Ah, you're awake. I'm preparing a feast for the two of us. You know...to welcome you home."

Malene stared at the dead body on the ground and felt sick again. She threw up yellow gastric acid. It burned in her throat.

"Don't look so outraged," Thomas said. "I didn't kill him. At least, I don't think I did, ha ha. I found him in a cave. I might have killed him. Who knows, right? At least we have something to eat."

Malene whimpered as Thomas picked up a piece of Mr. Bjerrehus and showed it to her. Blood was dripping from it.

"Looks delicious, don't you think?"

Malene shook her head and crawled backwards. She got up and started to run. She only made it a few steps towards the tunnel before Thomas yanked the chain forcefully and she fell flat on her face in the dirt.

III

DAY 11-12, OCTOBER 16TH -17TH 2014

EAT OR BE EATEN

47

WE WERE LOSING hope and, worst of all, we were running out of food. After eleven days underground, our bodies had started to change drastically. The skin now hugged the bones on our faces, and our ribs all showed. When we walked, our legs trembled. Knowing a lot about the subject, David had explained to me that without roughly a hundred and twenty grams of glucose a day, the human brain starts to malfunction and our bodies had started to eat our muscle mass. We slept constantly to not feel the hunger. Even our prayer time had stopped.

We never did find Malene or Mr. Bjerrehus, nor did Kurt ever come back from running off. I wondered what had happened to all of them, but didn't have the strength to look anymore.

On this morning on the eleventh day, I reached the bottom of the pit when I picked up an empty can of tuna and licked the inside again and again.

I had made another trade with Brian, and we still had a little water left, but none of us could go much longer without food.

Afrim's mother was doing the worst. She was all skin and bones and hardly awake at all anymore. I could see the anxiety in Afrim's eyes, and feared the worst. She had only a day or two more left in her, if that.

On the eleventh day, Brian came to us. He could barely walk as he came through the tunnel, flanked by Lars and Kurt, who apparently had joined them after running away from us. His wife, Annette, was happy to see him, but kept her distance. He smiled at her, but went to sit with Brian, not her.

"We've finally run out of food and water," Brian said, sitting down next to me. He had lost a lot of weight. "There is no more."

"No more water either?" I asked. "It was a big tank."

"Not big enough, apparently. Maybe there was another hole in it, I don't know, but the water is gone. We ran out of the last of the food this morning. And we're hungry."

"We all are, Brian," David said.

"Where is Thomas Soe?" I asked.

Brian shrugged. "We lost him some days ago. He was just gone when we woke up. We thought he would be back eventually, but he never showed up."

"Same thing happened to Mr. Bjerrehus and Malene," I said.

"You think they might have found a way out of here?" Kurt asked.

I shrugged. "Or they've gotten lost somehow. I don't know."

"It's strange," Kurt said. "I believe there's someone or something else in these tunnels. When I left from here, I wandered the tunnels for a day and a half. I heard strange noises, especially at night. Voices and singing. I heard footsteps and, I swear, someone was watching me while I slept. I woke up with a gasp and there was someone in the darkness with me. I swear there was. He was standing really close to me. I could hear him breathe. Thinking of what happened to poor Michael West, I started yelling and slamming my fist into the darkness, hoping to hit him. I did. My fist struck something and there was a sound like someone fell backwards. Then I heard footsteps, like someone running, and he was gone. I swear, I was certain he would have killed me."

"Could it be Mr. Bjerrehus?" Mrs. Sigumfeldt asked.

Kurt laughed. "No, he would certainly have killed me if he had the chance. He hates my guts as much as I hate his. You can be certain of that."

"Then, who else could it be?" I asked. "Thomas Soe? Malene?"

Kurt shrugged. "I don't know. People seem to go crazy down here. The lack of food and water makes us lose it. I tell you, we're going to end up eating each other."

"Speak of eating," Brian said. He nodded in direction of Afrim. "That dog still alive?"

"He's holding on like the rest of us," I said. I had a sense that this conversation wasn't going in a good direction. "Why?"

Brian shrugged. "Just wondering."

48

AFRIM SAW THE look on Mr. Jansen's face. It wasn't pleasant. He was staring at Buster with a strange smile, very similar to that of Afrim's aunt before she went to the hospital.

Afrim pulled Buster closer and held him tight. The dog was nothing but skin and bones. He could feel his ribs as he lifted him. Just like his mother. Afrim sniffled and looked at her. She hadn't spoken to him for two days. She had been awake for maybe a few minutes, in total, those same two days. Afrim knew she was doing poorly, and every day, he prayed to whomever would listen to please, please keep his mother and dog alive. But he knew there wasn't much time left.

Afrim watched as Mr. Jansen came closer. He sat next to Afrim and looked at Buster. "So, how's the dog?" he asked.

"Hhhe...he's alright," Afrim said.

Mr. Jansen touched Buster. He petted him on the back then felt his stomach. Buster didn't even move.

"Not much meat left on him, huh?"

Afrim shook his head, while staring at Mr. Jansen. He had never liked him much. Afrim had heard Mrs. Jansen screaming at night and Mr. Jansen yelling at her. She would scream for him to stop hitting her. Why he didn't stop, when she was obviously in pain, Afrim didn't understand, and he had asked his dad about it.

"Some men don't know how to appreciate a woman properly," he had told Afrim.

"Can't you teach him, Daddy? 'Cause she sounds like it hurts a lot," Afrim had said. "Why doesn't anyone help her? Everyone can hear her screaming, can't they?"

Afrim's father thought about his answer for a while. "Most people like to mind their own business. They don't like to meddle in other people's lives."

"But why? I don't understand." Afrim had asked.

His dad didn't have an answer. Later that same day, Afrim's mother had tried to reach out to Mrs. Jansen, and had asked her to come over for a cup of coffee, but Mrs. Jansen had told her she couldn't. Her husband didn't want her to be around *those Muslims*.

"She doesn't want our help, Afrim," his mother had said when she came back and slammed the door in anger.

So, they had done what everyone else in this neighborhood did. They had pretended they didn't hear her screams at night and moved on with their lives.

"He won't live much longer," Mr. Jansen said now to Afrim.

Afrim pulled Buster closer, so Mr. Jansen wouldn't touch him anymore. Mr. Jansen smiled, then got up and walked away. When naptime came and Afrim was supposed to go to sleep like the rest of them, he stayed awake and watched over Buster. Mr. Jansen was sitting at the end of the cave, keeping an eye on Afrim, while everyone else dozed off. When it was just the two of them, Afrim felt a chill roll down his spine. Mr. Jansen kept staring at Afrim and Buster, and then he got up and walked toward them again.

"Give me the dog," he whispered.

Afrim shook his head in desperation. "No. No. You're not getting him. He's my dog!"

"Sh, keep it down. We don't want anyone to wake up, now do we? Listen, kid. I know you love him, but he's going to die anyway. We might as well get something out of it. There's still meat on him. It could keep us alive for days. I tell you what, you give me the dog, and I'll split the meat with you. You can feed that mother of yours and help her stay awake. I have fire. We can roast the meat. It'll be much better than just watching him die. Either way, we'll eat him."

Afrim whimpered. He felt tears pressing on his eyes. The thought of anyone eating his dog made him cry.

"Please. Don't touch my dog."

"It's okay. He won't feel a thing. It's for a good cause. He'll keep us alive, remember? Keep your mom here alive so she can be with you when we get out of here."

Mr. Jansen reached over and grabbed Buster by his tail. He lifted the skinny dog into the air and smiled. The dog whined.

"What a nice piece of meat," he said.

"Please, sir. Please give me my dog back," Afrim cried. "I love Buster, please don't take Buster from me."

"I'll make sure to be quick," Mr. Jansen said, and grabbed Buster's neck. "I'll snap his neck quickly, so he won't feel a thing. It's the most humane thing to do, really. Put him out of his suffering. You don't want to watch him starve to death anyway, do you?"

Afrim cried harder. "Please…please, sir…please, don't…"

"Sorry, kid," Mr. Jansen said when another voice suddenly echoed loudly through the cave, waking up most of the people.

"Put the dog down!"

Mr. Jansen froze. So did Afrim. He couldn't believe his eyes. It was his mom. She had managed to push herself to her elbows and was looking at Mr. Jansen. "Give the dog back to my boy. It's all he has."

Other eyes were on them now. Rebekka was on her feet and approaching them. So was David.

"What's going on here?" she asked.

Mr. Jansen shook his head. "I'm not dying of hunger while the dog lives," he growled. "It could feed all of us. Think about it."

David pulled his knife. "Give Afrim his dog back."

"What? You're going to kill me over a dog?" Mr. Jansen said.

"Might as well," David answered. "You eat a lot more than the dog does."

Brian Jansen looked at Afrim. Afrim stared at Buster while crying.

"Screw you," Mr. Jansen said, and threw the dog to the ground. "Screw all of you. You'll regret it when we all starve to death."

"Buster!" Afrim yelled. The dog whined, then got back up on its feet and ran to him. Afrim was so busy taking care of his dog, he didn't notice his mother breathing in her last breath before her head fell to the ground with a loud thud.

49

"Mom? Mom? Please, wake up, Mom?"

Afrim's voice was breaking. So was my heart. I ran to his mother and felt for a pulse.

"Is she…?" David came towards us.

I nodded slowly. The light in Afrim's eyes went out. "No," he said, while shaking his head in desperation. "No!"

"I'm sorry, kid," I said, tears burning my eyes.

"NOOO!"

Afrim threw himself on top of his mother's dead body, crying and sobbing. "Don't leave me, Mom. Don't leave me down here. Please, come back. Please!"

I grabbed Afrim in my arms and pulled him away from the body, while David removed his mother and put her in with the others who had passed away.

It was hard for me not to burst into tears. I held Afrim tightly in my arms. I felt such a deep anger rise inside of me. I couldn't believe how unfair it was. I thought about my own children and cried even harder. They had to be missing their mother so much. Had they given up hope by now? Had Sune told them I was gone? Were they crying and sobbing helplessly like Afrim was?

I couldn't bear the thought.

"Shhh," I said, and put him on the ground with his back against the cold limestone wall. I stroked his hair gently. But it didn't matter. He was inconsolable. It wasn't until Buster came to him and crawled onto his lap that Afrim calmed down.

My eyes met David's as he returned. He had been crying too. His eyes were red.

"What took you so long?" I whispered, when he sat next to me.

"I had a meeting with God," he said. "Had to tell him how I felt about this." David clenched his fist. "I am just so…angry! I mean, of all the things I've been through lately…this is, by far, the worst. At least I was alone when I was kidnapped. It was just me, you know?"

"I know what you mean," I said.

Brian was sitting across from me, still scowling at the dog. I couldn't believe him. I felt so tired, but kept myself awake to keep an eye on him.

"Maybe we ought to sleep in shifts from now on," David suggested, when he saw me staring at Brian Jansen. "This guy isn't going to let go of this anytime soon. Others might get ideas as well. Hunger has that effect on some people. When faced with deathly hunger, all humanity ceases to exist. It's only about survival."

I threw a glance around the room and realized there was more than one set of eyes fixated on Buster. I suddenly wasn't so sure we would be able to protect him much longer, even though we had the advantage of having the knife. If there were enough people and they ganged up on us, we wouldn't stand a chance.

"Let's try that," I said. "You go first."

"Are you sure?" David asked.

"Yes. I'm too upset to sleep anyway. I'll be fine."

"Wake me up if they try anything, alright?" David said, and handed me the knife. I made sure everyone saw that I had the knife, then pulled Afrim and Buster closer to me, so they knew I would be protecting the two of them.

David leaned his head back and closed his eyes. For a minute, I envied him. I was so tired and really wanted to sleep as well. But I had a responsibility. I wasn't going to let Afrim down.

When David had been asleep for a few minutes, murmurs started among the men. I couldn't hear what they were talking about, but their debate was lively. Brian got up from his spot and walked across the ground. At first, I thought he was coming towards me and Afrim, and I clasped the knife in my hand, while preparing myself for the confrontation. As he came closer, Brian gave me a look, then walked right past me. Kurt and Lars followed him.

50

SHE COULDN'T STAND it anymore. She couldn't stand simply sitting there doing nothing while her stomach hurt from hunger and her son constantly slept because he had no more strength to stay awake.

With a deep sigh, Mrs. Sigumfeldt stared at the dog. She wasn't the only one eyeballing the dog, thinking it could keep them alive for a little longer. She was certain everyone in the cave was thinking the same thing. Except for that Rebekka woman and the handsome David Busck, who Mrs. Sigumfeldt remembered having seen on TV. He was much more handsome in real life. Even better looking than Michael West had been.

The bastard.

Tine Sigumfeldt couldn't believe he had abandoned her like that. Hadn't he cared for her at all? After all those years of coming to her house and sleeping with her when Mr. Sigumfeldt was away on business trips. Didn't they mean anything?

He never loved you, you fool. You were nothing but sex to him. He used you, that's all.

The thought made Tine Sigumfeldt angry. She had really

liked him. Him coming to her house had always been the highlight of the month for her. The kids never knew he was spending the night. She made sure he arrived when they were asleep and left before they woke up. But not on the morning of the collapse. That particular morning, Tine's youngest son, Frederic, had been awake early. He had knocked on the door to Tine's bedroom at five thirty and told her he had a bad dream. Tine had put him back to bed and tucked him in, but knew he wouldn't sleep. The dream had been too bad. Tine had to sit at his bedside, holding his hand until it was time to get up. Afterwards, she had sneaked back to her bedroom and told Michael West to wait till they had left the house to go to school.

It was strange how small decisions or coincidences ended up being so important...and some even fatal. His decision to leave all of them in the cave had been just that.

The bastard only got what he deserved.

Tine didn't finish the thought before she watched Brian Jansen and his gang get up and walk towards the dog.

If they eat that dog, I want in, she thought. *I want some too.*

She looked at Frederic, who was sound asleep, then back at Brian Jansen. To her surprise, he walked right past the dog, the two others following him.

Where are they going?

Tine Sigumfeldt stared at them as they disappeared out of the cave. She had a feeling they were up to something. She just knew they were. It was the same with her boys. Constantly out to get themselves in trouble.

Tine Sigumfeldt looked at her sleeping son once again, remembering how badly her husband had wanted sons. She had provided three of them, each time hoping in her quiet mind that it would be a girl this time. They had been so much trouble, almost to the point where she considered leaving all of them. It was just too much. She had been alone so much, since Mr. Sigumfeldt traveled for weeks at a time, sometimes ten days. Every time he had left her alone with the three kids, she had felt anger towards him. She had felt that he abandoned her. That was why she had decided to punish him by taking herself a lover. She felt she deserved it.

Tine Sigumfeldt stared after the three men once again. She couldn't help being curious. Where did they go? They had seemed so determined, like they had somewhere to go to, when there was nowhere for any of them to go. The few that had tried, they had never seen again. Michael West ended up dead. She looked at her boy.

He'll be fine. He won't notice you're gone.

Mrs. Sigumfeldt stroked his cheek, then got up and followed them into the tunnel. Even though she was in pain, she managed to move through the darkness, dragging her leg after her, hoping she could catch up with them.

As she walked through with her head bent, she saw a light at the end of the tunnel. It made her walk faster.

Maybe they found food? Maybe they know where to get water and just didn't want to tell the rest?

The thought made her smile. When she walked into the cave and found who was carrying the light, she didn't smile so much anymore. The eyes staring back at her from behind the flashlight were very well known to her. If she had known it would be her last word, she probably would have chosen it more carefully, but since she didn't, she simply said, "You?"

51

I heard a scream and jumped up, holding the knife out in front of me. That was when I realized I had dozed off, even though I had promised David to keep an eye on Afrim and his dog.

"What was that?" David said and opened his eyes.

"I don't know," I said.

Afrim was fine. Buster was fine.

"It sounded like it came from one of the tunnels," I continued. "Everybody alright in here?" I asked the others, who were now waking up and looking terrified at David and me. They too had been frightened by the sound.

"Mom?" Frederic asked. His voice was feeble. "Has anyone seen my mom?"

"I'll go check," David said, and took the knife from my hand. "Everyone else stay here."

"No. Let me," I said.

"Why?"

"If they come for the dog, I won't stand a chance. I need you to protect Afrim and everyone else in here. Only you can do it."

"If you say so," David said.

"I think that's best."

"Let me go with you," Kenneth Borges said. "I'm the one with most strength left, I think. You shouldn't go in there alone. That scream sounded serious."

"You'll need this," David said, and gave me the knife.

I took one last glance at the crowd left in the cave, while wondering what Brian Jansen and his gang were up to now. And where was Mrs. Sigumfeldt? Had she gone with them?

"Let's go," I said to Kenneth Borges, and led the way into the dark tunnel. We walked for a few minutes when I saw light coming from somewhere. I started walking towards it.

"You think it came from in there?" Kenneth asked. "But… but that's the grave chamber. That's where we leave the dead. I can smell it all the way out here. I don't think it's good for you to go in there. It's unsanitary."

Kenneth froze. I could tell he was afraid.

"Unsanitary or not, I have to check it out," I said. "Someone might be in trouble and need our help."

Kenneth grabbed my shoulder. "Those bodies have been in there for days. You don't know what kind of diseases have developed in there. There could be cholera and worse."

"I'll have to worry about that later. Besides, David was in there earlier today. If he is fine with it, then I'm fine too, but you can stay here if you like."

"I think I'd like that," Kenneth Borges said.

With the knife in my hand, I walked towards the cave that we had all been in at first, before we had managed to dig ourselves out and end up in the mines. I hadn't been in there since we left the dead bodies there and, to be completely honest, I felt scared to death by the thought of going in there. I usually didn't believe in ghosts or any supernatural things, but at that moment, I thought about the possibility of the screams coming from someone coming back from the dead. I clenched the knife in my hand as I walked closer, wondering if it would be enough to defend me. I took in a deep breath and ducked down to peek inside the hole. Then I froze. It wasn't a ghost; it wasn't the undead coming back to haunt us and take us with them to the land of the unliving. Whether what I saw was human or not, I don't know. It sure didn't feel like it. What I saw made me sick to my stomach. Inside the cave sat Brian, Kurt, and Lars. They were bent over the body of Afrim's mother, biting off chunks of her meat.

52

I couldn't believe what I was looking at. It looked like something out of a horror movie. I understood that hunger could lead people to do the strangest things, the most desperate things, but this?

I wanted to do something. I wanted to chase them away and let Afrim's mom rest in peace. I don't know if it was the look on their faces or what, but something told me if there was a fight, I wouldn't win. I gasped and backed up in terror till I was back where Kenneth was waiting.

"Let's get out of here," I said, and rushed past him, tears pricking my eyes.

"What was it?" Kenneth asked, as he came after me. "Did you see anyone? Was anyone in there?"

I felt sick just thinking about it again. I couldn't let go of those appalling images. "There was nothing there," I said. "Let's move on."

We took a turn into another tunnel and didn't walk long before another cave opened up. One I hadn't seen before. I wondered if the entrance to it had opened up in one of the latest collapses that still happened on a daily basis. I felt my way through the darkness only lit by the light of the cellphone I had taken with me. I was only pressing the button when it was necessary, to save the battery, since it was our last cellphone. I had been worried about us losing light completely. All we had left back in the big cave was the thick candle, and it was almost burned down by now. I wondered which would come first. The death from thirst or the loss of light? Were we just going to die in darkness?

I shook the thought and entered this smaller cave, followed by Kenneth. I gasped once again as I shone the sparse light around. On the ground, lay the body of Mrs. Sigumfeldt, or what was left of her. She had holes in her chest and face from something being poked through her.

"Oh, my goodness," Kenneth said, and held a hand to his chest.

I kneeled next to her body and looked at her wounds. They were thin, round, and deep…just like the ones I had seen on Michael West. Besides the wounds from something poking her, she was missing a lot of flesh on her stomach and arms. I lifted her arms and spotted marks on them.

"They look an awfully lot like teeth marks," Kenneth said, realizing the horror. "Oh, my God! Has someone…did someone…eat off her?"

I rose to my feet. "Like David said earlier, hunger brings out the darkest sides of man."

I felt anger rise in me while thinking about what I had seen in the grave chamber. The way I saw it, there was only one conclusion to this. Brian Jansen and his gang had killed Mrs. Sigumfeldt and eaten of her, then continued onto Afrim's mother. But did that mean they had killed Michael West as well? What about Malene and Mr. Bjerrehus? And Thomas Soe? Maybe they had started with him? Had they eaten him first, then moved on? But why would they leave

Mrs. Sigumfeldt to go eat from another body, when they clearly weren't finished with this one?

It made no sense. But, then again, none of their actions made much sense.

"Let's get back to the others," I said, and started backing up. I didn't want to touch the body or take it back to the grave chamber. All I wanted was to get the hell out of there…and fast.

"I think we need to get out of here," I whispered to David as we got back to the big cave. "Cannibalism has started to spread. It is only a matter of time before they'll take us down as well. "

"Brian Jansen?"

"Yes. I spotted him and the two others eating from Afrim's mother's dead body in the grave chamber. We found Mrs. Sigumfeldt killed and half eaten. I think we need to find a new cave somewhere to hide in."

"But some of the people can hardly move," David said. "They're too weak. I'm also worried about Afrim. His wound is infected. I just noticed it a few minutes ago. He let me take a look at it. He's in a lot of pain. He hasn't told anyone because he has been too worried about his mother. It's bad. He doesn't have long, if you ask me. If we move him, we risk making it worse. I think he has a fever."

I stared at Afrim, who was holding on to his dog. His small body was shaking and his eyes were shining feverishly. I felt a knot in my stomach. Was this the way it was going to be? Was everyone going to die, one after another, until there was no one left? I felt sad. I had come to care a lot for Afrim and Frederic, who was now also without his mother. I wasn't going to let them die. I would fight for them if I had to…fight Brian and his gang…kill them, if that was what it took to keep them away.

"We'll have to take our chances. It's the only way," I said.

"We can carry both of the boys, you and I. The dog will have to follow if it can."

I finished the thought, then felt tears roll across my face, just as Kenneth Borges suddenly yelled.

"Did you hear that? I heard something! Listen."

53

"Do you hear it? What a beautiful noise!" Kenneth was yelling...ecstatic. He grabbed me and spun me around. "Do you hear it? Eighteen years I have worked with drills like these. I can recognize the sound of a drill like that in my sleep."

When he put me back on the ground, I looked at David. He looked like he wasn't sure if the guy had lost it or if he had actually heard something. He was dancing back and forth between people in the cave telling them to listen.

"They're coming for us! They're coming for us," he chanted.

I tried to listen, but couldn't hear a thing. I guessed that Kenneth had simply lost it. After all, we were all bordering on insanity.

"Kenneth..." I said, wanting to tell him to calm down, that he was just hearing things...that he was imagining things that weren't there, but felt real to him. We had been through it before with others who thought they could hear drilling.

But, as I was about to finish my sentence, I heard it too. I heard the sound of something spinning, grinding, and hammering. It sounded very far away and, for a few seconds, I was certain I had started imagining things too, but slowly, hope grew in me. And soon I was as excited as Kenneth.

"It's true," I said, putting my ear against the limestone wall. "I hear it too. I really do."

For half an hour, the roar grew steadily louder, and around forty-five minutes later, David was ready to believe it too. It was unmistakably a drill, the sound traveling through thick layers of dirt and limestone.

"It's true, people. They really are drilling for us," I said to the rest of the crowd. Afrim smiled in his blushing feverish face. He hugged Buster. "Do you hear that, boy? They're coming for us."

"Now, it will take a while before they get to us," Kenneth said.

"How fast can a drill like that travel?" I asked.

"It depends on a lot of things, but I'm guessing they'll reach us within seven to ten hours," he answered. "We must be patient."

"I thought they had given up," Irene exclaimed. She had gotten up from her seat for the first time in days and was walking towards me on her trembling legs while holding onto her son, Benjamin.

"Me too," Kurt's wife, Annette, said. Her voice was breaking and she started crying, hiding her face in her arm.

"I hardly dare to believe it," Irene said, biting her lip. "Are you sure they'll be able to find us?"

"I...I hope so," Kenneth said. "It sounds like the drill is definitely getting closer by the minute."

I could tell he had his doubts as well. My head was spinning with this information. What if it stopped right above us? Oh, the terror of receiving a ray of hope. There was always the possibility of being disappointed. But it was still better than nothing. I was about to lose all hope in humanity down here.

"Should we get the others?" Irene asked. "Maybe call for them? Does anyone know where they went?"

I looked at David. I felt terrible. Then I looked at Frederic. He was soundly asleep. I hadn't told him about his mother yet. He hadn't been awake since I got back. David shook his head.

"I don't think we should tell them yet," he said. "Let's wait till they break through to the cave."

It was a decent answer, without me having to explain what I had seen. It would have been devastating to Afrim and Frederic if they knew. I didn't feel like anyone else needed to know…not yet, at least.

54

He kept calling her that name. Rikke. Malene wondered who Rikke was and why he insisted on calling her that. But she played along. For days, she played his little games and pretended she was that girl.

It seemed to make him happy, and it kept her alive.

She had refused to eat the meat he had served for them on the first day, but on the second, she couldn't resist it any longer. She was so hungry it hurt, and watching Thomas eat it with such delight made it even worse. She had to do it, she told herself. To survive. Just like she had to pretend like she liked Thomas Soe, like she had to pretend to be his girlfriend. Seven days had passed. Seven days she had counted by making marks on the wall at night when Thomas was asleep next to her. Seven days of being trapped with him...chained to his leg.

Every night, she wondered if there was some way she could get out. Every night, she lay with her eyes wide open and stared into the white limestone ceiling above her, wondering if she would ever get away.

The human meat made her feel nauseous, but it kept her

alive. And he had water. Thomas had plenty of water for her to drink. Slowly, she started to feel better physically; she regained much of her strength and started to think more clearly.

He was being nice to her. He would only slap her across the face if she wept and cried. He couldn't stand that, he said. He couldn't stand her whimpering. So, she only cried at night when he was asleep. He told her he would try and make her happy. That all he wanted was to get a second chance...that he was so happy she had decided to come back to him. He needed her.

"I need you, Rikke. I can't live without you. You know I can't," he said, over and over again.

The more she heard about this Rikke, the more Malene realized she had to have been that ex-girlfriend of his that he was once accused of having killed. Malene remembered the headlines on TV and the pictures of Thomas. At first, she had tried to talk to him about it, to tell him she wasn't Rikke...that Rikke was dead, but it made him so angry, she never dared to do it again. She learned to play along.

The body of old Sigurd Bjerrehus had started to smell and rot. It was a smell far worse than anything Malene had experienced before. Thomas had cut off so much meat from his body that you could barely tell it was the body of a human lying there on the ground, smelling. He had roasted the meat on his small bonfire to make sure it could last for a while. But now, they were running out. On the seventh day of her being trapped with him, they ate the last of the meat for lunch. She wondered what he would do next. They still had water for a couple of days more, but that would eventually run out as well. What was he going to do? She feared he would kill her and eat her next.

So, Malene had made an escape plan. Every night, while Thomas was sleeping, she thought about it, and tonight was the night. She knew where he put the butcher's knife. He put it in the same place every day on a small rock next to the old man's body. The chain between the two of them seemed to be just long enough. If she stretched out, she thought she might be able to reach the knife while he was still asleep. Maybe she could cut the chain with the knife. Maybe.

If not, then you'll have to kill him. You have to do it.

"You're not eating." Thomas looked at her with his head tilted. "You're not getting sick, are you? Rikke?"

She forced a smile. "I'm fine. Just tired, that's all."

Thomas smiled. His hands were shaking as he pushed the food closer to her. "Now eat, so you can get well."

Malene grabbed the meat and lifted it. It still made her sick to her stomach, knowing where it came from.

"That's it. That's my girl. Eat it," Thomas said. "You gotta eat to stay pretty."

The smell of the meat made the nausea worse. She closed her eyes and imagined she was with her mom and dad again, and that they were eating roasted chicken. Sophus, their dog, would sit next to the table, waiting for food to be spilled, or for her mom to feed him under the table, hoping no one would notice. Malene smiled, thinking of her family. She missed them so much. As she sunk her teeth into the meat and the juices filled her mouth with the taste of human flesh, she imagined herself in their arms again, hugging them, kissing Sophus, and playing with him like she did when she was a child.

"Good," Thomas said. "What is it they say? Eat or be eaten, right?"

Then he laughed.

55

It was the strangest of feelings. I was excited, hopeful, and at the same time, more anxious than ever. The mood in the cave had changed. The hope had changed them...had transformed the lethargy that almost bordered on apathy among the people. Those who barely spoke, were now talking amongst each other. Those who could walk were up on their feet, walking around, grabbing each other's hands, smiling, crying, and telling each other it was going to be all right...that they were coming for us.

I stood for a long time with my ear against the limestone wall, listening to the distant sound of the drill. Kenneth was right. It was the most beautiful sound in the world.

Now all we had to do was to wait patiently. The drilling continued into the afternoon. It felt like it was still unbearably far away.

"Do you think they'll come through tonight, or will we have to wait till tomorrow?" Irene asked Kenneth.

He shrugged. "I...I...it's hard to predict. The layers get more solid, the further down it gets. Might slow it down a little as it reaches the limestone."

"So, we should brace ourselves for one more night down here?" she continued.

"I would think so," he said.

It suddenly seemed like too much to ask of these people. I, for one, couldn't bear the thought of having to spend one more night down here. Not now that we had the hope that we would actually make it out. While Kenneth tried to assure everyone that it would be fine, but that they had to be patient, and it would take time before they would be able to get them out of there, I was suddenly struck with a horrendous fear.

What if they never break through? What if it stops? What if it passes us? What if they miss?

"I can't stand it," Annette said. "The air down here is so tight. I need fresh air. I need to see trees. I need to feel a breeze on my face. I can't stand one more night down here, I simply can't!"

"Well, you have to."

The voice was Brian's. My heart stopped, and I turned to look. Brian, Kurt, and Lars had come back. Their faces were still smeared with dried up blood and dirt. I kept seeing them bent over Afrim's mother's body.

Oh, the horror. They've come back to kill all of us and eat us, haven't they? Starting with Afrim's dog!

Brian grumbled and walked past me. He sat down on the ground. "It's gonna take a long time before that drill comes through," he continued.

Annette looked at Kurt. "Sweetie? Did you hear it too?" she asked. "They're coming for us."

Kurt sighed deeply. Then he nodded. "Yes. We heard it too."

Annette smiled widely. "Good. Do you want to sit over here with me?"

I could tell Kurt was arguing with himself. He took one more glance at Brian, then made his decision.

"I'd like that."

Lars threw himself next to Brian. I walked up to Afrim and sat next to him and Buster. The dog wagged its tail. I petted it gently on the head. It looked like it wasn't going to last much longer. Brian cast a glance at Frederic, who was still asleep. I didn't like the way he looked at him and I pulled the boy close to me. I felt his pulse. It was very weak.

"I say we sue someone once we get out of here," Brian yelled. "Let's sue the city or whomever built this neighborhood. Kenneth, you said you tried to warn them, right? Maybe you could be our star witness?"

Kenneth nodded. "Yes, I did. I told them the earth underneath is limestone, that limestone erodes over hundreds of years, creating these holes underneath us. When the limestone erodes, it forms pockets, like these we're sitting in. Sinkholes are depressions or a collapse of the land surface as the limestone below cracks and develops fractures. Acidic waters seeping through the soil lead to the breakdown over long periods of time. We just had a high accumulation of rainfall in a brief period of time and that is, in my opinion, why the collapse happened at this time."

Brian smiled. "See. That's what I'm talking about. We could become millionaires after this. I say we get ourselves some great lawyers and sue the bastards. Someone has to pay, that's for sure."

"Let's get out of this place first, shall we?" David argued. "It is a little ridiculous to talk about money and lawyers while we're still trapped down here."

Brian grumbled, annoyed. I agreed with David. It seemed wrong to think about going to court and settling scores when we were still buried alive underground.

56

He had gotten the idea when looking at a map of the area, he told Martin. It was while lying awake at night, wondering if Rebekka could somehow still be alive.

"That's when it hit me," he said, his eyes sparkling with hope. They were standing in Martin's hotel room that morning, eleven days after the collapse. Martin was packing up. They were going to live with Mathilde's mother until the insurance company found them a temporary house to live in. Martin had finally given up hope of ever seeing his baby brother again. They had told them they had stopped looking for survivors, and now their only concern was the ground's stability. They were only drilling samples and lowering cameras into the ground to examine the deeper layers of the soil. They wanted to make sure the rest of the surrounding areas weren't going to collapse as well. That's why they had started drilling further away from the crash site. They were very sorry, they had told them, but there was no way there could be any survivors anymore; it was simply impossible, and they weren't able to recover their bodies without risking the ground collapsing further. That was the message they had given Martin, and he had chosen to believe it. There was no use in fighting it anymore. David was gone, so was their house, and all their belongings. It was over. They had to find a way to move on from here. He had just talked to Mathilde about how he looked forward to getting away from this place and never coming back, when Sune knocked on his door. Sune put the map on the table and showed him.

"Monsted Kalkgruber is the world's largest limestone mine. It covers sixty kilometers of tunnels underground, six stories in thirty-five meters depth. But, that's only what they know about. I read a lot about it online and an underground like that might have many pockets and tunnels that might spread further out and deeper down than what we think."

"Like, over here where our neighborhood used to be?" Martin said.

"Over time, the limestone erodes and creates these pockets or caves underground. That's why the collapse happened. But if Rebekka and the rest could in any way be alive, it would be by hiding in those caves and tunnels."

Martin looked at the map, then at the papers Sune had printed them out from the limestone mine's webpage, showing the caves and tunnels and telling how you could get a guided trip down into the mine and watch a movie of how they used to mine the limestone.

"There are only eight hundred meters of tracks made for visitors. Only two kilometers have lights. The rest is all just a lot of dark tunnels and caves."

"Like an underground maze," Martin said pensively.

"You said it yourself on the first day the two of us met," Sune said. "You wished there was another way. Well, if there is another way to find them besides digging, then this is it."

Martin had no idea what to say. Could this really be a possibility? Could they have survived down there in those caves and tunnels for this long?

He shook his head. "No," he said. "There is no way they could have survived this long without water. Let's face it. It's over."

Sune shook his head. "Come on. Let's give it a try. Let's walk down there and see what we can find. I can't do it alone, and the police and firefighters won't help. I tried all morning down at the site to explain this to them, but they say it's over, that everyone is dead, and then handed me a card to an emergency psychologist if I needed to talk to someone. Come on, Martin. You're my only hope."

Martin looked at the map again. "How will you even do this? You said it yourself. There are only lights in two kilometers of the tunnels. We have no idea how deep this goes down. We could easily get lost ourselves. For what? The chances we could find them are so small, almost non-existent. I have a family, Sune…a child and a wife I have to take care of."

"And I have three children, but I'm not giving up. I want them to see their mother again."

"It could take days to even get down there," Martin argued. He had closed that door, and really didn't want to have to open it up again. Hope was such a deceitful matter. He really didn't want to get disappointed again. He didn't want to hope anymore. He wanted closure.

Holding their baby in her arms, Mathilde came forward. "I think you should do it," she said.

Martin looked at her. She had never been more graceful than in this moment.

"This is the way to get proper closure," she continued. "If you give up, you'll always wonder."

Martin stared at his beautiful wife and baby. What had he done to deserve such an understanding and caring wife?

"Who's going to take care of your kids while we're gone?" he asked Sune.

Sune smiled happily. "My father-in-law is here to help."

57

WE WENT TO SLEEP. Well, most of us did. I, for one, couldn't sleep. I didn't dare to after what I had discovered about Brian Jansen and his gang. I felt like I had to keep an eye on them, and so I did. David stayed awake with me, holding the knife in his hand. Our last cellphone died a few seconds before it was time to sleep. Now, all we had left was a candle that had almost burnt out. Kenneth wore a watch and kept track of time for us. He told us we should get some sleep right before he went down himself.

"They won't be drilling at night," he whispered.

As the drilling faded, I felt myself losing hope again. I wanted them to keep at it, I wanted the sound to remain inside the walls. The sound fading caused me to panic slightly, and for a few seconds, I felt like I couldn't breathe.

"Are you okay?" David asked.

I looked at him, gasping for breath. Then I started crying. I couldn't help it. He put his arm around me and hugged me. "It's okay, Rebekka. It'll be okay. They're coming for us, remember? Now, you listen to me. They will come for us. I know they will. When I was kidnapped somewhere in Syria, that's what I told myself every day, every hour. Someone will come for you. Your family will pay the money they are asking. Even when I heard about other prisoners who had been decapitated and the videos of it sent out for the entire world to see, I stayed hopeful. I told myself that would never happen to me…that I was a survivor. You have to tell yourself that. You've survived eleven days down here. You can get through one more night. I know you can."

I nodded and calmed down. "Thanks. I needed that."

"I know it's scary. We're so close, but so much can still go wrong. Believe me, I know. It was the same thing when they came for me, put a bag over my head, and threw me in the back of their truck. I hoped and prayed I was going to be released, but so much could have gone wrong. They could decide to not live up to their end of the agreement. They could decide they didn't care at the last minute. But I was released. I was left on the side of the road, kicked and beaten, but they left me, and I came home. I came home. You'll get home too. You'll get to hold that baby of yours again."

I had no idea where he got the strength. I was impressed by him, to put it mildly.

"Now, I want you to get some sleep," David continued. "I'll keep an eye out on Afrim and Buster and whoever else might need my help. Don't worry. You need sleep, Rebekka, or you won't make it."

I put my head in his lap and felt more secure than I had in a very long time. He stroked my hair gently, and soon I dozed off as well.

The drill broke through in the early morning hours. I had slept heavier and better than any other night underground, when I was awakened by a loud crash. Startled, I jumped up.

"They're coming through!" David yelled. He got up. "Wake up, everyone. It's finally happening!"

"I can't believe it," I said, and stood next to David.

While others joined us, we watched as more dirt fell into the cave from the hole they were creating.

David put his arm around me and held me close. "Me either," he said. His voice was breaking, and I could tell he was moved. The grinding and pounding sound of the drill became extremely loud as it came through.

"Get ready, folks," Kenneth said. "Don't stand too close. It's going to burst through now."

There was a small explosion, followed by the sound of rocks tumbling to the ground. The grinding of metal against rock stopped, and was replaced by a whistle of escaping air. A big pile of dirt had landed on the ground. We looked up to see what looked like a pipe peeking inside of our cave. A drill bit inside the pipe was lowered and rose and lowered again.

"They've realized that the bit has entered an empty space," Kenneth said. "Now they're cleaning the shaft."

The drill bit continued to be lowered, then risen again. I felt a desperation in my body. What if they didn't know we were here? How should we tell them?

"Shouldn't we knock on the drill or something?" I asked. "Maybe with your knife, David."

"Good idea," Kenneth said. "Do it now that the drill has stopped."

David walked closer and started knocking on the drill bit. He was pounding it with all the strength he had left. Then, he stopped, and we listened to see if they would reply by pounding back.

But no sound came. Nothing but silence until the drill was suddenly removed again.

"It's going back," Annette screamed desperately. "It's going back up and they don't know we're here!"

58

MALENE WAS HOLDING her breath, trying hard not to cry. She had managed to grab the knife and had been working on the chain for hours now. Desperately, she pounded the butcher's knife on the chain to try and cut it off, but every time she swung it and hit the chain, it would make a loud noise, and Malene was scared she would wake up Thomas. He had been in a bad mood all afternoon, and she had to wait for hours for him to finally fell asleep. She looked at her watch that had a little light in it if she pressed the button on the side. It was close to seven in the morning. Thomas would probably wake up soon. Desperately, she swung the knife against the chain again with a loud grunt. The knife slammed into the rock beneath it, and left a visible mark on the chain, but it wasn't enough.

"Just one more time," she whispered.

She lifted the knife again, when suddenly she heard someone. She paused with the knife in mid-air and listened. There it was again. Someone was screaming. The sound bounced off the walls. It sounded like a woman. Come to think of it, it sounded like several people. They were yelling and screaming.

It had to be the others from the big cave. Were they still alive? Were they so close that she could hear them screaming?

If so, then she would actually have a chance. If only she could find her way back to them. Malene let the knife hit the chain once again and felt how the blade slid right through. She gasped and looked at the split chain.

I'm free!

Thomas seemed to still be deeply asleep. With her heart pounding in her chest, she started walking backwards, fumbling her way towards the tunnel leading out of Thomas' cave. Her eyes were fixated on the sleeping Thomas as she stepped inside the tunnel and started running. The tunnel soon became narrower, and she bent her head as she ran. In the distance, she could hear the voices of people yelling and screaming.

They can't be far. Just keep going. Keep running. You'll find them. Just get away from here.

Malene was panting, stumbling, and forcing her legs forward through the tunnel with the butcher's knife in her hand. She reached the end of the tunnel and entered a cave. She lit her small light in her watch to see better. There were many exits. She counted them. There were five to choose from.

Now what?

She spotted a mark on one of them. She remembered David telling them he had marked the dead ends with an X. That had to be one of them. But then she remembered how Thomas had told her that he had changed them. He had made new marks, making it look like it was really a dead end when it wasn't, and so on to keep the others away. If that was so, then this wasn't a dead end. But, was it the right one? Would it lead her back to the others?

She thought she heard something and turned with a gasp.

She pressed the button on her watch again. "Who's there?" she asked.

No answer. Could it have been a bat?

She breathed heavily, then made her decision. Thomas could come after her any second now. She walked into the tunnel marked with the X and started running. As she was about halfway through, she heard footsteps behind her. She gasped and turned, but couldn't see anything.

"Who's there?" she asked again.

It's all in your head. You're being paranoid, Malene. You're wasting precious time. You need to keep moving. He'll be after you as soon as he knows you're gone. He'll kill you. Run!

Malene turned and ran with all the strength she had in her. Luckily, she had been eating a lot and had enough water to drink, so she was strong. Strong enough to run.

She reached the end of the tunnel and ended up in another cave. As soon as she entered it, she knew she was alone. It was one of the bigger caves. One of those the size of a small church with high ceilings. Every time she moved, it made a loud noise that echoed off the walls. She heard something behind her and turned with a loud gasp. She couldn't see anything, but knew there was someone there.

Malene fumbled with her watch to be able to light it up to see. Suddenly, a flashlight was turned on right in front of her and the beam lit up a face. It was Thomas' face. He was grinning.

"Where do you think you're going, *Rikke?*"

59

I couldn't believe it. My worst nightmare had come true. They were pulling the drill back up, and we had no chance to tell them we were down here. Annette and Irene were screaming and yelling. The rest of us turned to Kenneth, like he should somehow offer us an explanation.

"I...I guess they..." he stopped. I could tell he didn't know what to say. He simply shrugged.

"They weren't even looking for us, were they?" I asked.

"I...No. This kind of drill is used for taking samples of the underground," he said.

"So, there's no chance they even heard me pounding?" David asked.

"I don't think so. But, hey...here's to hoping, right?" Kenneth said, trying to sound cheerful.

I felt hope run off me like shampoo in the shower. "So, you're saying there's still a chance?" I was trying, even though I could feel that I had already given up. This was it. They weren't going to find us. I breathed hard and deeply to try not to panic. Annette was still screaming into the hole the drill had left.

"It's no use," Kenneth explained to her. "They won't be able to hear you. It's too far away. We're too deep underground."

The drill pulled out of the hole and left a small ray of light coming from it. A breath of fresh air oozed into our cave and hit me. I closed my eyes and breathed in, while imagining trees and lakes and birds and flowers. I tried to look up, but couldn't see anything. Soon, the ray of light disappeared and I stepped away. Annette looked up.

"Something is coming down!" Annette yelled. She moved away in a hurry.

"What?" I said and rushed back to see. As I came up to her, something peeked inside the hole and looked at us.

"What is that?" Annette asked.

"It...It looks like a small camera," I said.

Kenneth and David came closer and looked at it as well.

"It *is* a camera," Kenneth said. "They use it to take pictures of the underground. Probably to see how big the empty space is that they hit. Now, gather everyone around. Let's wave!"

I felt like crying. We were like children jumping up and down, waving, yelling, and laughing. I couldn't hold my tears back. I jumped into David's arms and hugged him. He hugged me back. He was very quiet, but I could tell he was crying as well. We stood like that for quite a while until we let go and turned to hug the others. I went to Afrim and kneeled next to him and Buster.

"Hold on, kid," I said. "It won't be long now till they get us out of here. Keep the faith."

"Good," he said sniffling. "I don't think Buster can hold out much longer. He stops breathing sometimes."

The dog was skinny. He looked like one of those abused dogs you see on TV sometimes.

"He better stay alive," I said, trying to sound optimistic. "We haven't come this far for him to give up now."

ELEVEN, TWELVE ... DIG AND DELVE

I leaned over and kissed Afrim's forehead. He was still burning up. His leg had become badly infected.

I walked to Frederic, who had been asleep for a long time now without waking up. I was very worried about him and felt his forehead. It was clammy, but ice cold. His pulse was weak. This wasn't good.

"You hold on too, kiddo," I whispered. "Don't give up. Not now. Not when we're this close to getting out of here."

60

He had to punish her. Of course he did. There was no other solution, Thomas thought to himself, while looking at the girl. She was standing in front of him, holding out the knife and threatening him with it.

"Come on, you sick bastard. Come on if you dare!" she yelled, while poking the knife towards him.

Thomas chuckled. It was almost funny to watch her.

"What are you doing?" he asked.

"I'll kill you. I swear I will," she growled.

It amused Thomas to watch her move around...like a small fairy or a ballet dancer tiptoeing back and forth while groaning when she tried to poke him. Thomas chuckled again and made sure to move if she got too close. She was so adorable.

Now, don't forget she tried to leave you again. Don't let her deceive you. She must be punished!

Thomas shut off the flashlight, and they were now in complete darkness. The girl whimpered.

"Turn it back on, you bastard!" she yelled.

Thomas stood completely still and waited. He could hear

her small feet moving across the ground. Then he heard her grunt and imagined her trying to poke at him with the knife, but reaching nothing but air. Thomas was very good at moving quietly. He held his breath and followed the sound of her footsteps. Moving fast, he grabbed her around the waist from behind and lifted her in the air. The knife fell out of her hand and dropped to the ground with a loud clank.

Thomas lit the flashlight again, took in a deep breath, grabbed her hair, and pulled her to the ground. Then he kicked her and slammed the flashlight into her back. Malene screamed as he slammed it at her again. Something broke when the flashlight hit her leg. It sounded like it was the bone.

"Stop! Thomas, Stop!"

He grabbed her shoulder and turned her over so he could look at her when he slammed his fist into her face again and again. Then he lifted her head and stroked her gently over her bloody face.

"Why did you leave me? Huh? Why do you keep doing these things to me? Why Rikke? Why? You know I have to punish you. Just like the last time when you left me for that guy, now that was a mistake, huh?" He paused to laugh goofily. "I was so happy to finally have you back, and then you go and do it to me again. We could have such a wonderful life together. Why do you insist on ruining it?" He shook his head with a tsk. "You don't see it yourself, do you? You're so self-destructive. You should be very happy to have me in your life. I'm just trying to protect you. Don't you see that?"

The girl spat in his face. "You're insane! You're sick, Thomas!"

Thomas wiped away the spit, then looked at her, trying hard to not let her spite get to him.

"You know I hate to do this to you, but I have to," he said, and lifted his fist and slammed it into her face once…twice… and then a third time. The girl's nose was bleeding heavily.

Her eyes rolled back in her head. She was sobbing. Thomas held her by her neck and looked at her for a long time, just watching the blood. He followed a drop that rolled from her nose, across her lip, and ended in her mouth. He wondered what it tasted like. Then he leaned over and licked it. The girl opened her eyes with a gasp and tried to push him away. He held her down forcefully and enjoyed watching her squirm underneath him.

"Stop," the girl screamed, almost panicking. "Just stop, you fucking bastard. Get off me."

"I'm beginning to think you like this," he said, moaning. "How else am I to explain why you keep doing this? Why you keep putting yourself in this position. I think you like it. I think you enjoy me beating you, don't you?"

Thomas was the one who enjoyed it. He loved feeling his power, feeling how easy it was to hold her down against her will. She was like a child that needed discipline and he could give her that. Just like his own mother had done to him.

"Please," she sobbed. "Won't you please just let me go? Please just leave me alone."

"I'm sorry," he said smiling. "No can do."

61

She could see the knife. It was lying on the ground not far from her. If she could just…if she could only stretch her arm a little further, she would be able to get it. Thomas seemed to have forgotten all about it.

"Don't ever leave me again!" he screamed into her ear so loud it hurt, then slammed his fist into her chin. The pain struck through her head and neck.

"Please…please stop."

But she knew he wasn't going to. She was trying to push him away with her hands, but wasn't strong enough. He was on top of her now, holding her down with his weight. She tried to kick and scream, but knew it was no use. He was way too strong for her. Her only hope was that someone would hear her screams in the tunnels and maybe come look for her. But she knew they were all terrified of going into the tunnels after what happened to Michael West. If they weren't afraid of getting killed, then they were afraid of getting lost.

Malene stared at the knife that was only a hand's length from the tip of her fingers. It wasn't far. Carefully, Malene wiggled her body sideways every time she kicked and tried to get Thomas off. Slowly, she was getting closer, her fingertips were so close to the blade.

Just a few inches more.

She knew what she would do once she reached the knife. She would stab him. She would kill him in cold blood. She had made her decision. She had never killed anyone before, or even thought about doing it, but Thomas, she could kill. After all he had put her through, she was certain she could do it. She just wished she had done it the first time she had the chance.

"Look at me," Thomas said.

He was shining the flashlight in her face, and she had to close her eyes. She was certain she could feel the blade barely touch the tip of her middle finger.

Just a little more.

"Look me in the eyes!"

"I can't," she said. "Not when you point that flashlight at me."

He lowered the light and she opened her eyes again. Now her fingertips were definitely touching the knife. She stared into his eyes. He grabbed her chin and held it tight.

"Can you promise me you won't try to leave me again?" he asked.

Malene squirmed to the side one last time, and finally grabbed the tip of the blade. Now she was able to pull it. It slipped out of her fingers.

Damn it.

She wiggled her fingers and got a hold of it again.

Thomas slapped her face. "Promise me!"

"I promise, I promise!" she yelled.

He stroked her face. "Good girl." Then he turned his head and shone the flashlight on her hand that had reached the blade of the knife. His facial expression changed. His eyes went black.

"What the hell?"

Grab the knife and turn it, hurry up!

"Were you just lying to me?"

Now, Malene! Get ahold of the knife before he kills you!

But Malene couldn't get a proper grip on the knife. When her hand closed on it, she cut herself on the blade, and had to let go. Thomas stood up, then kicked the knife to the side. He walked back towards her. Malene whimpered. She didn't like the look on his face.

"Please," she cried.

Thomas walked closer. He bent over her. "Now, why do you keep deceiving me? Why do you have to do that? Now I have to hurt you again, Rikke. I have to. Don't you see that you make me do this to you?"

"Pleeease..."

He lifted her by the collar of her shirt.

"I'm sorry," he said. "But I have to do it."

What happened next, happened so fast, Malene hardly saw it. She was looking at Thomas, waiting for the flashlight to hit her in the face. One moment he was there, bent over her with his angry flaming eyes, the next he was gone. She lifted her head and found him with his back up against the limestone wall, a fire poker pierced through his chest. On the other end of the poker stood a woman.

"Run, little girl," the woman yelled. Run!"

So she did. Malene sprang to her feet and realized one of her legs was broken. It hurt like crazy. But she managed to get out anyway, dragging the bad leg behind her. She got through one tunnel, then entered a cave and into another tunnel. She walked in a daze of shock and desperation, wondering how to get away. She had no idea where she was going, and knew she would end up dying in those tunnels, but then she suddenly heard a sound. She stopped in fear as someone approached her in the darkness.

"Who's there?" she said, her voice shaking in fear.

What if it's Thomas? What if he survived somehow and escaped?

But it wasn't Thomas. The voice answering was one she knew, one she knew she could trust.

62

THE CAMERA WAS removed after we had been waving for about an hour, and soon something else was lowered into the hole through the pipe. A plastic bottle fell to the ground.

"It's a letter!" Annette yelled. "There's a letter inside of it."

I picked it up and opened the bottle. My hands were shaking when I unfolded the paper and read it out. It simply said:

We know you're down there. Hold on tight and we'll get you help.

I looked at David and smiled. Everyone around us was cheering loudly. Even Brian Jansen.

"We're getting out," I said, my voice cracking with joy.

Can this really be? Are we really being rescued after all this time?

"You'll see your babies," he said.

I hugged him again. He held me tightly in his arms.

"I can't believe it," I said, almost crying with joy.

"Me either," David said.

It was the strangest feeling of euphoria that spread among us. Everyone was hugging each other, many were crying, and some laughing, but it didn't last very long. Our happiness was suddenly broken when we heard a loud scream coming from one of the tunnels. The screaming continued. It sounded like it was distant, but it was always hard to tell in those mines.

My heart stopped.

"What is that?" David asked.

"I don't know," I said. "I'm afraid someone is in trouble."

"Should we do something?" he asked. "Form a patrol and go see what it is?"

I stared at him. Part of me wanted to say no, for the simple reason that I couldn't bear any more misery. Not in this hour of happiness. I wanted to celebrate, not go into the tunnels and find more dead, half-eaten bodies.

Irene suddenly pulled my shoulder. "Have you seen Benjamin? Have you seen my son?"

I turned to look around in the cave. "No. I remember seeing him earlier. He was just here."

"He *was* here right before when the letter came through the pipe. He kissed me on the cheek and hugged me after you read it out loud. I spoke to Annette, and a few minutes later I turned to look for him, and he was gone. Did you see where he went?"

I shook my head. "No. I'm sorry. But I'm sure he'll be back soon. Don't worry." But I had suddenly started to worry. Everyone else who had left suddenly had never come back. Michael West, we had found; Mrs. Sigumfeldt, I found. Mr. Bjerrehus and Malene were never found, but I had a feeling they had both been killed inside those tunnels, just like Michael West and Mrs. Sigumfeldt, and I had a feeling I knew who had done it.

I threw a glance at Brian, who was hugging Kurt's wife Annette in happiness. Could he have kidnapped Benjamin? Forced him to go somewhere with him just to kill him? As far as I knew, Brian, had been here all the time. It didn't seem possible. I was puzzled. The screams stopped just as suddenly as they had started. David and I looked at each other again. I had no idea what to do. There was no way we could not react to this. There was no way I could ever live with myself. Especially not now that we knew we had a chance of actually surviving.

A thud made me turn and look. Something was shooting through the hole in the ceiling and landing on the ground.

"It's water," Kurt yelled. "Bottles of fresh water."

The bottles kept falling down through the pipe. I ran to grab one myself and drank greedily. David did the same. Never had water tasted this good.

"More is coming." Annette yelled. "It's food!"

Packs of crackers fell through the pipe and landed in a pile on the ground. I counted at least ten packages. We threw ourselves at them and ate. I hadn't forgotten about the screams, but at that point, I had to think about my own survival.

More food came through the hole, this time it was a loaf of bread, then another and another. Up to maybe twenty loaves of bread, then some fresh fruit…bananas, enough for everyone and deliciously juicy apples.

"Remember to eat small portions," David told everyone, drawing on his own experience from coming back from Syria. "Your body needs to get used to being fed again. Slowly increase the portions over the coming days."

I drank mostly water and ate some crackers, then topped it off with a banana, and then I was full. I looked at David.

"Now that we have some strength, do you think we should go check who was screaming?"

He nodded. "We'd better."

Just as we got up to get going, someone entered the cave.

"Hey, can I get a little help here?"

It was Benjamin. In his arms, he was carrying Malene.

63

"I heard her scream and ran through the tunnels towards the sound," Benjamin said, and put Malene on the ground with David's help.

"I met her in one of the tunnels. She was so scared. I spoke to her gently and told her it was just me. Then, she fainted, and I had to carry her back."

"I wonder where she's been all these days?" I asked, and examined her. She was in a very bad state. Her face was bruised and swollen; her leg looked like it was broken.

"Someone beat her badly," David said. "She needs medical attention."

"But how?" I asked.

He sighed. "I don't know, but we have to somehow tell them on the surface. We have several who need to see a doctor soon."

Benjamin's mother Irene brought him water and food. He ate greedily while looking at Malene.

"You did a good thing saving her, son," Irene said.

Benjamin looked worried. "Will she be alright?"

"Not if she doesn't get to a hospital soon," David said.

ELEVEN, TWELVE ... DIG AND DELVE

He walked to the pipe and tried to yell into it. "We need help! Someone is badly hurt!"

I looked at Afrim. Kenneth had made sure to bring him water and food. But he wasn't doing well either. He was mushroom-pale and shaking. He tried to smile while clinging onto his dog.

It suddenly occurred to me that maybe we did have contact with the outside world, but we weren't in the clear yet. We were still buried deep underground.

Something was lowered through the pipe. We went to take a look at it.

"It's a telephone receiver," Kenneth said. He grabbed the earpiece and listened.

"We need help," he said. "Medical help. Someone is badly hurt."

He listened. We all crept closer, like we thought we would be able to listen in as well. My heart was pounding in my throat. Kenneth didn't look happy.

"But...but we need help now. People are hurt!" he said angrily. "We can't wait that long. How..."

He stopped to listen again, then removed the earpiece, and looked at all of us. It didn't look good.

Uh-oh!

"I'm sorry, my friends," he said. His voice was breaking. "It's going to take a while for them to dig us out."

"How long?" asked Lars. The tone in his voice was angry.

"Maybe a month."

A month????

The news made Annette start to scream. Brian was yelling. Someone was crying; others were grumbling angrily. I stared at David, then at Afrim, Frederic, and Malene.

There is no way they will survive that long down here.

"What are we going to do?" I asked David. I held back my tears, but it was hard. This was brutal. It was more than I could take. I couldn't even find it in me to be happy that I might see my kids again. Not when I knew Afrim wouldn't ever get to come with us. Neither would Frederic or Malene. Or Buster, for that matter. How was I ever going to live with myself?

"Why can't they do it faster?" I heard Brian Jansen ask Kenneth, almost attacking him like it was his fault.

Kenneth took a couple of steps backwards. Brian was acting aggressively towards him. I pulled David's shoulder, so he could be prepared to step in if it was necessary.

"I...the ground is too unstable...they're afraid it'll crash in on us," Kenneth tried to explain. "They have to be careful."

"So, they expect us to just stay put down here for a month, huh? Being fed like animals at the zoo?" Brian asked.

"Let's not...Let's try and stay calm, shall we?" Kenneth said, but Brian had him pinned up against a wall now. David interfered.

"Stop it, Brian," he said. "We're all in the same boat here. Let go of Kenneth."

Brian looked angrily at Kenneth, then let him go. He grunted as he passed David and me, pointing his finger at us. "I've about had it with you two. You better sleep with one eye open from now on."

64

THEY HAD REACHED the part of the mines where they ran out of tracks, and soon there was no more light either. Martin and Sune had prepared for that and brought flashlights and plenty of batteries. Sune reached into his pocket and pulled out his phone. There was no signal, they were now completely out of reach. They had spent the entire day yesterday preparing for going into the mines on their own. They had researched everything there was to know about the mines and the underground, then gone to a shop and bought the right equipment to be able to survive for days. They had brought lots of water and food. They had warm sleeping bags, rope, knives, and pickaxes. They were wearing hiking boots and, most importantly of all, they had brought paper and a pen to map the mines so they wouldn't get lost. There were two underground lakes in the mines, but no one had ever gone deeper than that, so there was no map, and no one knew what was waiting for them down there. For all they knew, they might run into a dead end, and that would be it.

But at least they would have tried.

Martin felt optimistic, even though he knew the odds were

against them; even though it was a long shot, and even though everyone was probably right that they were all dead. Maybe Martin was just refusing to admit that his brother had died. Maybe they were right about that. But he just couldn't let the thought go...that *what if*. What if he was still alive underground in the mines somehow?

"We have to go to our right here," Sune said, and looked at the only map they had managed to get ahold of. The top level of the mines was usually open to the public, but only in the summer. The rest of the year, it was closed to let the bats live and breed in peace. It was a certain rare type of bat that lived in the mines that had to be preserved. Other than that, the mines were only used for conserving cheese from one of the biggest cheese manufacturers in Denmark. *Riberhus oste* let their cheeses ripen inside the tunnels at one of the top levels for three weeks, because of the constant temperature and moisture in there. They were, apparently, perfect conditions.

"We'll get to one of the lakes in a few minutes," he continued. "After that follows the second one, and then we're on our own."

They went through a tunnel and ended in a big chamber where the lake was. It was cold and clammy in there. Sune put on a jacket. Martin did the same. They had still only reached the top layers of the mines. It was believed that they continued six layers down. That's what they knew of, but Sune and Martin had spoken to a local engineer who had told him that it was only a guess. No one knew exactly how deep they went or how far the tunnels spread. In his opinion, they shouldn't have been allowed to build houses so close to the mines in the first place. He had a colleague who had tried to warn the city about it for years, he told them.

"We believe he fell in the hole with the rest of the neighborhood," he said. "He was out there taking samples when the crash happened. He had been keeping an eye on the area for a long time, never would give up. I guess he was finally right in the end. Guess being right is highly overrated after all."

The lake was right in front of them now. It was stunning. The cave was as high as a cathedral, and the water reflected their flashlights. They continued on dry land past it and by the time they saw the second lake, they stopped to get a sip of water from their bottles.

"As soon as we enter that tunnel over there, we're on our own," Sune said. "No maps, no help to be had. Are you ready for that?"

Martin nodded. He was scared, but hopeful. This felt good. Finally, he felt like he was actually doing something instead of just watching from behind the police blockage. He was finally trying to really help his brother.

"I'm ready," he said, and put his backpack back on.

Sune smiled and nodded. "Let's go then. Let's go find them."

IV

DAY 15, OCTOBER 20TH 2014

THE ONLY WAY IS UP

65

THE MOOD IN the cave was unbearable. No one spoke anymore. Most were simply sitting with their backs against the wall, waiting. We had been in this state for three days now. It was evening again, and yet another night was ahead of us in the cave. They had lowered a big lamp for us that was lighting up the entire cave. I hated when it was time to shut it off and go to sleep. The nights seemed endless in the darkness.

Was this what we were going to do for the next month? Simply sit here and wait? Wait while some of us might die?

I sat next to Afrim and put my arm around him. He was burning up. I could tell by the look in his eyes that he knew he wasn't going to make it. They had lowered medicine for the fever, but it didn't help. The infection was too bad. Buster was panting heavily. He was short of breath and his heart was beating fast. He had hardly touched the water I had given him. He too knew he was running out of time.

Brian Jansen was constantly eating. He refused to listen to David's advice on taking it slow for the first few days. It looked like he was afraid he was never going to get fed again. Even though they kept throwing food down the pipe several times a day. It was the strangest thing. All of a sudden, getting water and food enough was no issue. It dawned on me how fast your circumstances could change. And you along with it. People in the cave had started to change. They were quarrelling and snapping at each other. I couldn't blame them. The waiting was a drag.

Benjamin was sitting with Malene. He was concerned about her, and didn't leave her side. I wished I could give him good news, but there wasn't any to give. His mother brought him a bottle of water, and he wet Malene's lips using his finger. I couldn't stop wondering who had hurt her this badly. We had all been in the cave when we heard the screams, hadn't we? Could someone have snuck out? And where had she been for more than a week? She seemed well nourished. Had she found food somewhere, before encountering whoever beat her?

The earpiece was lowered every day when they wanted to speak to us. Basically, they told us the same thing every day. They were still working on getting us out, but we had to be patient. Every day, the same damn story. They asked us if we were all right. We told them three kids were almost dying; they told us they were working as hard as they could, but we had to be patient. There was nothing they could do to make it faster.

The earpiece was lowered again. This time Kurt took it.

"Hello? This is Kurt. Kurt Hansen. I used to live in number eleven. If we're still fine? Well, it depends on how you see it. How many? Well no one has died since yesterday, if that's what you're asking me. There are still twelve of us left. Yes, we lost some that survived the crash. Some got lost in the mines; we don't know what happened to them. What? Let me just ask a second."

"Hey, listen up, everybody," he yelled. "Apparently, we've become some kind of celebrities up on the surface. There are journalists that want to talk to us, does anyone want to say something to them?"

Brian jumped up. "Give me that," he said, and pulled the earpiece out of Kurt's hand. "Yes, this is Brian Jansen. I used to live in number five. Yes, I'm good, but I want to get out of here. Why aren't we getting out? What do you mean you don't know? You're just a journalist from a newspaper? Then go ask them why we're not getting out faster. Lord knows we've been here long enough. What did you say? Spokesperson? Yeah, definitely. More like a leader. Yeah, I guess you could say I've been kind of the leader of the pack down here. Yes, you can quote me saying that. TV deals? I don't know. Who's saying anything about that? Aha…aha…yes, well I guess I might be interested. Oh, they're talking about making a movie as well, are they? Well, I might be interested in helping them. Yes, I am the man they should discuss the rights to our story with."

We all looked at each other. Lars got up and walked towards Brian. He reached out to grab the earpiece. Brian pulled away.

"I want in on this," he said, and reached out for the phone again.

Brian didn't let him take it. "I'm talking to them," he said.

"Give it to me. You're no more the leader down here than I am," Lars said.

"Who said any of you are the leader?" Irene said. "I say Rebekka is the leader."

Please leave me out of this. I don't want anything to do with it.

Irene looked at me. "You talk to them," she said. "You'll make a great deal for all of us. I want you to represent me."

"Nonsense," Brian said. "I'm a better negotiator. I was born to lead." Brian returned to the conversation in the earpiece while holding Lars back with his hand. "No…no, we're not quarreling down here. We're fine. You tell any TV producer, reality show, or movie producer that we're willing to talk money. Lots of money. Have them ask to talk to Brian and no one else. Now, goodnight." With a grin, he let go of the earpiece and it was pulled out of the pipe.

Lars clenched his fists and looked at Brian.

"You better not try and cheat any of us out of the deal," he said.

"Easy there, buddy. I'll take good care of all of you; I'll even make you rich. The journalist told me they are very eager to get all of us in on TV deals and reality shows; anything about *the trapped twelve* is in high demand. Yes, that's what they call us. Isn't it great?" Brian Jansen slammed his hands together with a satisfied grin.

I wasn't sure if he was still grinning after the lights suddenly went out.

66

"What happened?"

Kurt yelled in the darkness.

"Hey! Who turned out the lamp? It's not time to go to sleep yet," Lars yelled. "We still have a couple of hours left. Turn the light back on."

I moved towards the place where I knew the lamp was, while wondering what had made it go out, who had made it go out, when I heard a yell and a loud thud, sounding like someone falling to the ground. Then there was a yell and a gasp.

"What the hell?"

It sounded like Brian.

I reached the lamp and turned the knob. The light immediately went back on. The first thing I saw was Brian Jansen. He was up against the limestone wall with a strange expression on his face and a fire poker pierced through his chest. Blood was flowing from the wound to the ground.

"Oh, my God!" I exclaimed and cupped my mouth.

Right in front of him, still with the fire poker between her hands, stood a woman I recognized from the day of the collapse. She had been in the street debating with Mrs. Sigumfeldt.

"Mrs. Jansen?" Afrim yelled with terror in his voice.

The woman didn't answer. She grunted and growled, while looking into the eyes of her husband, who was pierced on a fire poker. David sprang to her and grabbed her. He pulled her away. Brian looked perplexed. He stared at the blood and the big hole in his chest where the fire poker was still stuck. He tried to speak, but nothing but blood spluttered out of his mouth. I looked into his eyes and saw the horror when he realized that this was it. Everybody stared, paralyzed, at him, while he slowly and painfully left this earth.

"Don't pity him!" Mrs. Jansen screamed like a wild beast, while David held her down. "He's only getting what he deserves. Like the rest of them."

Kurt approached her. "What have you done, Gitte?" he asked. "You killed him. Why?"

"I should have killed all of you. You and this neighborhood. You think I don't know what you did, huh? You think I don't know? You closed the curtains on me. You and your wife. You didn't want to look at me. You didn't want to see. You are all monsters!"

"What are you talking about?" Annette asked.

"Like you don't know. That Saturday night three months ago when I was in the street, asking for help, ringing all the doorbells, and screaming. No one helped me. No one cared enough. I was bleeding…there was blood running from my… running down my legs because of that…pig over there." Gitte Jansen was sobbing heavily now. I was trying hard to keep track of her story and what was going on.

"He hurt you?" I asked. "And then you ran for help?"

"He beat me. But there was nothing new about that. Everyone knew that's what he did. But, that time, he kicked me in the stomach."

Gitte Jansen had a hard time breathing. David let go of her. She bent over and started crying hard.

"He kicked you in the stomach?" I asked.

She lifted her head and looked at me. "I was with child," she whispered.

Annette and Kurt gasped.

"Don't give me that," Gitte Jansen said. "You knew. You all knew."

Annette kneeled in front of her. "I didn't know," Annette said. "I swear, I didn't know."

"Then why did you leave me out there in your front yard? I was crying for help. I had no phone. I needed an ambulance. I saw you in the window. I saw all of you. You closed your curtains, so you didn't have to look at me."

"I…" Annette looked at Kurt for help.

"We thought you were drunk," he said. "It was late. You were screaming and acting crazy. We thought you were high on those pills you sometimes take. They make you do things like that. It wasn't the first time. I swear, we didn't see the blood. Annette wanted to help, but I told her not to. I told her to leave you alone. I can see now that it was wrong."

"I'm so sorry," Annette said. She was about to cry.

"You said they all got what they deserved," I said. "Did you kill others down here?"

Gitte Jansen nodded. "Mr. Bjerrehus, Michael West, and that bitch, Tine Sigumfeldt. They all played a part in me losing my child. See, Brian was in the house; he had kicked me out, so when I realized I was bleeding, the first place I ran to was my neighbor across the street, Mr. Bjerrehus. There was light in his windows. I pounded on his door, and rang the doorbell, yelling for help, but he didn't open the door. I saw him, though. I saw him standing in the window, right before he closed the curtain on me. I couldn't believe anyone could be that cruel. When I realized I wouldn't get any help from him, I ran down the street. Mr. and Mrs. Frandsen weren't home, so I passed their house and ran to knock on Mrs. Sigumfeldt's door. I knew she had her lover visiting, that Michael West guy, who has a wife and a kid across town. I rang the bell and screamed for them to help, but they did the exact same thing. They looked at me from the window, then closed the curtain. I ran from door to door, but no one helped. It wasn't until I reached the Berisha's house, sweet little Afrim's parents' house that I received help. They called for an ambulance right away. But when I reached the hospital, it was too late. I lost my child."

"So, when you hit Mrs. Sigumfeldt's car that morning and blocked the road, I take it that it wasn't an accident?" I said.

"Hell no. I wanted that bitch to suffer for what she had done to me. But I got my revenge later on down here. I was trapped for a long time under the debris of a house. Once I managed to dig myself out, I found a lot of stuff. I found food and water bottles enough for a long time, along with a flashlight, and I found this fire poker. I grabbed it, thinking I could use it for digging if I needed to, but one day, while exploring the tunnels, I saw you. I saw all of you. I heard voices and followed them. Then I saw you in this cave. I was so angry. It occurred to me this would be the perfect place for my revenge. Even though I was going to die down here as well, at least I would get my revenge. No one would ever question me afterwards. No police would ever come after me. Ha. I even ate some of Mrs. Sigumfeldt, just to stay alive, after I had run out of food."

"So, you were the one, not Brian?" I asked, puzzled. It began to make sense.

She nodded.

"I had to. To survive."

"But did you also beat up Malene?" I asked.

"No. Thomas Soe did that. The bastard. Beating the crap

out of the poor girl. It doesn't matter. He's gone now. Take my word for it."

Okay, I thought to myself, trying to get the story straight. So, Gitte Jansen was the one who had been killing people in the tunnels, not Brian. It made a lot of sense. I turned to look at his dead body, still pierced into the limestone wall. People around Gitte Jansen were in shock, staring at her with eyes wide and hands covering their mouths. What a mess. It was unbelievable. I was happy that we had finally figured out what had been going on in the tunnels, but I was puzzled to know how we were supposed to stay down here for yet another month with a murderer in our group. How were we to keep her from killing more people?

67

I couldn't sleep at all that night. We had decided to take turns sleeping, David and I. We had to keep an eye on the sick and on our prisoner. David had tied her hands with some rope the surface had provided us. It had come in a survival case that contained a lot of things, among them, a first aid kit, a knife, and a rope.

David came to me and sat down. "You're supposed to sleep," he whispered.

"I know," I said. "I just can't."

"Too many thoughts, huh?"

"A lot of questions and things I simply don't understand, yes."

"It's a lot to take in at once, this story," he said.

"You can say that again. Now, I wonder how we're supposed to make it an entire month. Don't you think she'll try and escape? If she does, we'll never find her again. It seems like she knows the tunnels better than any of us."

David shrugged with a soft smile. "I don't know. Let's just say that then we have a new situation. We'll deal with it if it gets to that."

ELEVEN, TWELVE ... DIG AND DELVE

I smiled. I liked that about David. He didn't worry. He took things as they came…if they came his way. It was a rare quality in people.

"You think they'll start digging the hole tomorrow?" I asked.

They had told us they would need to dig a big shaft to get us all out of, and that was why it was going to take a long time. But, much to our frustration, they hadn't even started yet. And it had been three days already. It was devastating. I thought about Sune, Julie, Tobias and William and suddenly missed them terribly. I felt so sad thinking about what they had to be going through. They had probably heard by now that I was alive, but that they had to wait a month to be able to see me again. How did that make them feel? Was it as unbearable for them as it was for me? We had asked if we could speak to our relatives, but they hadn't granted us that permission yet. They just said they'd *look into it*. Kenneth said that they might be afraid to let people, especially children, into the crash-site, since they weren't very sure of the stability of the ground. The thought didn't make me particularly comfortable…to think we had made it this far and then it might all crash on us anyway.

We'll deal with it if it gets to that.

David could tell I was sad and he put his arm around me. He pulled me closer and held me in his warm embrace for a long time. I enjoyed it and closed my eyes. He talked to me about his family, about his brother and parents, about him growing up and how his brother had always been there for him, how he had always gotten him out of trouble.

I had finally dozed off when someone entered the cave. The last person I would ever have expected to see down here.

"Rebekka?"

68

I stared at Sune, while still being held in David's arms.

"Sune?"

He was dirty and seemed tired. But it was definitely him. Next to him stood a guy I had never seen before.

"David?" the guy said.

David let go of me and we turned away from each other like children caught kissing in the schoolyard.

"Martin?" David said. "Is that really you?" Then he laughed joyfully.

It was so hard to believe that it was anything but an illusion caused by too much time spent underground. I blinked my eyes, thinking I might have finally lost touch with reality and started seeing things that weren't there.

"Rebekka. It's me," Sune said, and came towards me.

I still needed time to digest this and make sure he was real.

"But…what? What…how did you…where did you come from all of a sudden?" I asked. I realized I could ask questions later, then rushed towards him to feel if he was actually real. I threw myself in his arms. Yup. He was real. He grabbed me and hugged me.

ELEVEN, TWELVE ... DIG AND DELVE

"My God. Thank God you're alive. I thought I had lost you, Rebekka. I thought you were gone."

"Me too. I thought I was about to die. How did you find us?"

"We walked through the mines. It took three days," Sune said.

"And a lot of luck," the guy David was hugging said. "Hi, I'm David's brother Martin."

I shook his hand, still holding onto Sune's arm with the other. I wasn't going to let go of him again.

"Heard a lot about you," I said. "I'm Rebekka."

"I know," Martin said. He had tears in his eyes. We all had. Mine rolled across my cheeks.

"The kids, how are the kids?" I asked.

"They're with your dad," Sune said.

"My dad? But, is he well enough to take care of them?"

"If you ask him, he is. I told him I thought you might have fallen into the mines and could be alive down here, but that everyone else didn't believe us, so we had to go in alone. He never hesitated once. Never told me it was impossible or tried to talk me out of it. All he said was he would take care of the kids for as long as it took."

"Sounds like him," I said. I looked into Sune's eyes. He looked so tired. I could only imagine how bad I had to look after this long underground.

"We've got food," I said, and showed him the bundle of food that had been lowered to us. "They finally broke through the ceiling three days ago, but they say it'll take a month to dig us out."

"Well, now they don't need to," Martin said. "We mapped the entire way here. We can get you back in three days."

"Less than three days," Sune said. "We took a couple of wrong turns on the way and ended up in dead ends. A lot of the tunnels have crashed and are blocked. But it's all on the map now." Sune kissed me on the lips. How I had longed to feel him this close again. It felt incredible.

"We have sick people that need help," I said. "We'll have to get them out of here as soon as possible. And we need to carry them. Three of them can't walk on their own; they're too sick."

Sune nodded and looked at them. "Let's get to it, then," he said. "Let's wake everyone up and begin the hike. The sooner we leave, the better. It's almost morning anyway."

V

DAY 19, OCTOBER 24TH 2014

GOING HOME

69

It took exactly two and a half day for us to get to the surface. It was a terrible hike. We took turns carrying Malene, Frederic, Afrim, and Buster, but it takes a lot of strength to carry another human being, especially when you are as weak and feeble as we were. We had to take many breaks to make sure everyone would make it. I was scared all the way for Afrim, whose fever was getting so bad he lost consciousness just before we reached the entrance to the mine. Never in my life had I been happier to see sunlight and the bright blue sky than in the first seconds I stepped outside. Even the clouds were beautiful and oh…oh the trees. Their orange and brown colors were astonishing. And the fresh air…oh, the fresh air. It felt like the best thing in the world to be able to breathe in fresh air. I guess it is true. You only know how to fully appreciate it when you've been deprived of it.

As soon as we had reception, Sune managed to call for assistance, and soon the entrance to the mine was crowded with paramedics and police.

We were all taken away in ambulances and admitted to the hospital in Viborg for observation. Just to sleep in a real bed again was amazing. It's hard to explain how little things suddenly meant the world to me.

The next day, Sune brought the kids to see me. I had never been happier than when I finally held my babies in my arms again. I cried and kissed them, then cried some more. It went on for hours.

"You're so skinny, Mom," Julie said. "I hardly recognized you."

"Well then, I guess you and I should eat a lot of cake in the coming days; what do you think?"

But she wasn't in the mood for jokes.

"I thought we'd lost you, Mommy," she said seriously.

"I know. I thought so too," I said, and pulled her close. I looked into her beautiful eyes. She was so strong and not so little anymore.

William didn't understand much. He was glad to see me and hugged and kissed me, but didn't seem to understand much else. Julie, on the other hand, was devastated.

Tobias was quiet for a long time. He hid behind Sune. I signaled for him to come closer then gave him a warm hug.

"I was so scared down there. Scared of never getting to see you again," I said.

"I knew you'd make it," Tobias said. "I told Dad you never give up."

"Well, I'm glad he didn't give up either," I said, while I leaned over and kissed him.

Later that afternoon my friend Lone paid me a visit. We cried a lot and she told me she had been so afraid to never see me again.

"Next time you'll visit me in Karrebaeksminde instead. How about that?" I said and hugged her.

When she had left I went to see Afrim and Buster in their hospital room. They had managed to kill the infection and put his leg in a cast. He was going to keep his leg, the doctor told me, even though it had been close. He had responded well to the antibiotic and could already sit up in his bed. Afrim's father was sitting next to him, holding his hand, when I entered. Afrim smiled and Buster wagged his tail when they saw me. Afrim's father got up and greeted me.

"Thank you so much, Rebekka," he said. "Afrim told me all you did for him and how you helped him and protected him."

"Well, he did most of it himself," I said, and winked at him. "He and Buster make quite the team."

I hugged Afrim. "Thank you," he whispered.

"You're welcome, kid," I said.

I petted Buster on the head. I couldn't believe he had survived. He was one tough cookie.

"I bet you can't wait to get back to Karrebaeksminde?" Afrim's father said.

I smiled and shook my head. "Well, yes and no. I'm leaving a part of my heart behind. An experience like this is not something you ever forget. Neither are the people you shared it with."

"Come and visit us soon," Afrim yelled after me as I left.

I was discharged later that day and walked past Frederic's room, just to check on him. I saw his dad, Ole Sigumfeldt and his two brothers sitting by his bed, while Frederic was sitting up in the bed. I didn't go inside. It looked like more of a family moment. Just to see that he was all right was enough for me.

"Ready to go home?" Sune asked. I nodded. I had seen the two boys were all right, and I knew Malene would be too. Benjamin had come by my room earlier that day and told me she was much better, and that he finally had the courage to ask her out on a date. I knew Mrs. Jansen was in the hands of the police, so she was someone else's headache now. All the people who had lost their homes would be relocated into barracks outside of town, for the time being, they were told. I felt bad for all of them. They had survived being underground, but their trouble hadn't ended yet.

I looked at Sune and my wonderful children. I looked down the hall and wondered about David. He had left the hospital that same morning without saying goodbye to any of us, I had been told. I wondered if I would ever see him again.

Then I turned and looked at my family. All were smiling faces.

"I've never been more ready."

THE END

Do you wanna know what happens next?

Get Thirteen, Fourteen…little boy unseen here:

GRAB YOUR COPY TODAY!

Dear Reader,

Thank you for purchasing *Eleven, Twelve...Dig and Delve*. After reading this book, you might be wondering whether these sort of limestone mines are real. I can tell you, they are. In Denmark, we have a few of them. Monsted Kalkgruber is, in fact, the world's biggest limestone mine, and most of what I tell about them in this book is true, including the fact that they ripen cheese inside of them. You can see their web-page and see pictures from inside the mines here: http://www.monsted-kalkgruber.dk/da.

Rebekka and Sune are going home to Karrebaeksminde now, but I am far from done with them yet. There will be more books about them and their adventures in the future. Until then, don't forget to check out my other books by following the links below. And don't forget to leave a review of this book if you can. It means the world to me.

Take care,
Willow

To be the first to hear about new releases and bargains from Willow Rose, sign up below to be on the VIP List. (I promise not to share your email with anyone else, and I won't clutter your inbox.)

- Tap here to sign up to be on the VIP LIST -

Tired of too many emails? Text the word: "willowrose" to 31996 to sign up to Willow's VIP text List to get a text alert with news about New Releases, Giveaways, Bargains and Free books from Willow.

Follow Willow Rose on BookBub:

AFTERWORD

BB Follow me on BookBub

Connect with Willow online:
Facebook
Twitter
GoodReads
willow-rose.net
madamewillowrose@gmail.com

BOOKS BY THE AUTHOR

MYSTERY/HORROR NOVELS

- In One Fell Swoop
- Umbrella Man
- Blackbird Fly
- To Hell in a Handbasket
- Edwina

7TH STREET CREW SERIES

- What Hurts the Most
- You Can Run
- You Can't Hide
- Careful Little Eyes

EMMA FROST SERIES

- Itsy Bitsy Spider
- Miss Dolly had a Dolly
- Run, Run as Fast as You Can
- Cross Your Heart and Hope to Die
- Peek-a-Boo I See You
- Tweedledum and Tweedledee
- Easy as One, Two, Three
- There's No Place like Home
- Slenderman
- Where the Wild Roses Grow

JACK RYDER SERIES

- Hit the Road Jack
- Slip out the Back Jack
- The House that Jack Built
- Black Jack

REBEKKA FRANCK SERIES

- One, Two…He is Coming for You
- Three, Four…Better Lock Your Door
- Five, Six…Grab your Crucifix
- Seven, Eight…Gonna Stay up Late
- Nine, Ten…Never Sleep Again
- Eleven, Twelve…Dig and Delve
- Thirteen, Fourteen…Little Boy Unseen

HORROR SHORT-STORIES

- Better watch out
- Eenie, Meenie
- Rock-a-Bye Baby
- Nibble, Nibble, Crunch
- Humpty Dumpty
- Chain Letter
- Mommy Dearest
- The Bird

PARANORMAL SUSPENSE/FANTASY NOVELS

AFTERLIFE SERIES

- Beyond
- Serenity
- Endurance
- Courageous

THE WOLFBOY CHRONICLES

- A Gypsy Song
- I am WOLF

DAUGHTERS OF THE JAGUAR

- Savage
- Broken

ABOUT THE AUTHOR

The Queen of Scream, Willow Rose, is an international best-selling author. She writes Mystery/Suspense/Horror, Paranormal Romance and Fantasy. She is inspired by authors like James Patterson, Agatha Christie, Stephen King, Anne Rice, and Isabel Allende. She lives on Florida's Space Coast with her husband and two daughters. When she is not writing or reading, you'll find her surfing and watching the dolphins play in the waves of the Atlantic Ocean. She has sold more than two million books.

Connect with Willow online:
willow-rose.net
madamewillowrose@gmail.com

HIT THE ROAD JACK- EXCERPT

For a special sneak peak of Willow Rose's Mystery Novel *Hit the road Jack (Jack Ryder Book 1),* turn to the next page.

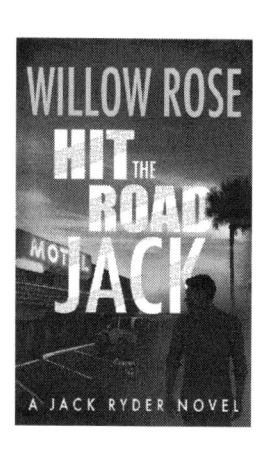

This could be Heaven or this could be Hell
   Eagles, Hotel California 1977

PROLOGUE

DON'T COME BACK NO MORE

1

MAY 2012

She has no idea who she is or where she is and cares to know neither. For some time, for what seems like forever, she has been in this daze. This haze, in complete darkness with nothing but the sounds. Sounds coming from outside her body, from outside her head. Sometimes, the sounds fade and there is only the darkness.

As time passes, she becomes aware that there are two realities. The one in her mind, filled with darkness and pain and then the one outside of her, where something or someone else is living, acting, smelling and…singing.

Yes, that's it. Someone is singing. Does she know the song?

…What you say?

The darkness is soon replaced by light. Still, her eyes are too heavy to open. Her consciousness returns slowly. Enough to start asking questions. Where is she? How did she end up here? A series of pictures of her at home come to her mind. She is waiting. What is she waiting for?

…I guess if you said so.

Him. She is waiting for him. She is checking her hair in the mirror every five minutes or so. Then correcting the make-up, looking at the clock again. Where is he? She looks out through the window and at the street and the many staring neighboring windows. A feeling of guilt hits her. Somehow, it seems wrong for this kind of thing to take place in broad daylight.

...That's right!

A car drives up. The anticipation. The butterflies in her stomach. The sound of the doorbell. She is straightening her dress and taking a last glance in the mirror. The next second, she is in his embrace. He is holding her so tight she closes her eyes and breathes him in until his lips cover hers and she swims away.

...Whoa, Woman, oh woman, don't treat me so mean.

His breath is pumping against her skin. She feels his hands on her breasts, under her skirt, coming closer, while he presses her up against the wall. She feels him in his hand. He is hard now, moaning in her ear.

"Where's your husband?" he whispers.

"Work," she moans back, feeling self-conscious. Why did he have to bring up her husband? The guilt is killing her. "The kids are in school."

"Good," he moans. "No one can ever know. Remember that. No one."

...You're the meanest old woman that I've ever seen.

He pushes himself inside of her and pumps. She lets herself get into the moment, but as soon as it is over, she finds herself regretting it...while he zips up the pants of his suit and kisses her gently on the lips, whispering, *same time next week?* She regrets having started it all. They are both married with children, and this is only an affair. Could never be anything else, even if she dreamt about it. The sex is great, but she wants more than just seeing him on her lunch break. But she can never tell him. She can never explain to him how much she hates this awkward moment that follows the sex.

"They're expecting me at the office...I have a meeting," he says, and puts his tie back on. "I'd better..."

...Hit the road, Jack!

She finally opens her eyes with a loud gasp. The bright light hurts her. Water is being splashed in her face. She can't breathe. The bathtub is slippery when she tries to get up. Her eyes lock with another set of eyes. The eyes of a man. He is staring at her with a twisted smile. She gasps again, suddenly remembering those dark chili eyes.

"*I guess if you said so...I'd have to pack my things and go,*" he sings.

"You," she gasps. Breathing is hard for her. She feels like she is still choking. She is hyperventilating. Panicking.

The man smiles. On his neck crawls a snake. How does that old saying go again? *Red, black, yellow kills a fellow?* This one is all of that, all those colors. It stares at her while moving its tongue back and forth. The man is holding a washcloth in his hand. She looks down at her naked body. The smell of chlorine is strong and makes her eyes water.

"You tried to kill me," she says, while panting with anxiety.

I have to get home. Help me. I have to get home to my children! Oh, God. I can hear their voices! Am I going mad? I think I can hear them!

"I guess I didn't do a very good job, then," he answers. His chillingly calm voice is piercing through every bone in her body.

"I'll try again. *That's right!*"

2

MAY 2012

She had never been more beautiful than in this exact moment. No woman ever had. So fragile, her skin so pale it almost looked bluish. The man who called himself the Snakecharmer stared at her body. It was still in the bathtub. He was still panting from the exertion, his hands shaking and hurting from strangling the girl. He felt so aroused in this moment, staring at the dead body. It was the most fascinating thing in the world. How the body simply ceased to function. And almost as fascinating was what followed next. The human decaying process. It wasn't something new. Fascination with death had occurred all throughout human history, characterized by obsessions with death and all things related to death. The Egyptians mummified their dead. He had always wished he could do the same. Keep his dead forever and ever. He remembered as a child how he would sometimes lie down in front of the mirror and try to lie completely still and look at himself, imagining he was looking at a dead body. He would capture cats and kill them and keep them in his room, just to watch what would happen to them. He wanted so badly to stop the decaying process, he wanted them to remain the same always and never leave.

The Snakecharmer stared at the girl with fascination in his eyes. He caught his breath and calmed down again. He still felt the adrenalin rushing through his veins while he finished washing the girl. He washed away all the dirt, all the smells on her body. He reached down and cleaned her thoroughly between her legs. Scrubbed her to make sure he got all the dirt away, all the filth and impurities.

Then, he dried her with a towel before he pulled her onto the bathroom floor. His companions, his two pet Coral snakes, were sliding across her dead body. He grabbed one and let it slide across his arm while petting it. Then he knelt next to the girl and stroked her gently across her hair, making sure it wasn't in her face. Her blue eyes stared into the ceiling.

"Now, you'll never leave," he whispered.

With his cellphone, he took a picture of her naked body. That was his mummification. His way to always cherish the moment. To always remember. He never wanted to forget how beautiful she was.

He dried her with a towel. He brushed her brown hair with gentle strokes. He took yet another picture before he lifted her up and carried her into the bedroom, where he placed her in a chair, then sat in front of her and placed his head in her lap.

They would stay like this until she started to smell.

PART 1

I GUESS IF YOU SAY SO

3

JANUARY 2015

He took the dog out in the yard and shut the door carefully behind him, making sure he didn't make a sound to wake up his sleeping parents. It was Monday, but they had been very loud last night. The kitchen counter was still covered with empty bottles.

At first, Ben had waited patiently in the living room, watching a couple of shows on TV, waiting for his parents to wake up. When the clock passed nine, he knew he wouldn't make it to school that day either, and that was too bad because they had a fieldtrip to the zoo today and Ben had been looking forward to it. When they still hadn't shown up at ten o'clock, he decided the dog had to go out. The old Labrador kept sitting by the door and scraping on it. It had to go.

So, Ben took Bobby out in the backyard. He had to go with him. The yard ended at the canal, and Bobby had more than once jumped into the water. Ben had to keep an eye on him to make sure he didn't do it again. It had been such a mess last time, since the dog couldn't climb back up over the seawall on his own, so Ben's dad had to jump into the blurry water and carry the dog out.

The dog quickly gave in to nature and did his business. Ben had a plastic bag that he picked it up with and threw it in the trash can behind the house.

It was a beautiful day out. One of those clear days with a blue sky and not a cloud anywhere on the horizon. The wind was blowing out of the north and had been for two days, making the air drier. For once, Ben's shirt didn't stick to his body.

He threw the ball a few times for the dog to get some exercise. Ben could smell the ocean, even though he lived on the back side of the barrier island. When it was quiet, he could even hear it too. The waves had to be good. If he wasn't too sick from drinking last night, his dad might take him surfing.

Ben really hoped he would.

It had been months since his dad last took him to the beach. He never seemed to have time anymore. Sometimes, Ben would take his bike and ride down there by himself, but it was never as much fun as when the entire family went. They never seemed to do much together anymore. Ben wondered if it had anything to do with what happened to his baby sister a year ago. He never understood exactly what had happened. He just knew she didn't wake up one morning when their mother went to pick her up from her crib. Then his parents cried and cried for days and they had held a big funeral. But the crying hadn't stopped for a long time. Not until it was replaced with a lot of sleeping and his parents staying up all night, and all the empty bottles that Ben often cleaned up from the kitchen and put in the recycling bin.

Bobby brought back the ball and placed it at Ben's feet. He picked it up and threw it again. It landed close to the seawall. Luckily, it didn't fall in. Bobby ran to get it, then placed it at Ben's feet again, looking at him expectantly.

HIT THE ROAD JACK- EXCERPT

"Really? One more time, then we're done," he said, thinking he'd better get back inside and start cleaning up. He picked up the ball and threw it. The dog stormed after it again and disappeared for a second down the hill leading to the canal. Ben couldn't see him.

"Bobby?" he yelled. "Come on, boy. We need to get back inside."

He stared in the direction of the canal. He couldn't see the bottom of the yard. He had no idea if Bobby had jumped in the water again. His heart started to pound. He would have to wake up his dad if he did. He was the only one who could get Bobby out of the water.

Ben stood frozen for a few seconds until he heard the sound of Bobby's collar, and a second later spotted his black dog running towards him with his tongue hanging out of his mouth.

"Bobby!" Ben said. He bent down and petted his dog and best friend. "You scared me, buddy. You forgot the ball. Well, we'll have to get that later. Now, let's go back inside and see if Mom and Dad are awake."

Ben grabbed the handle and opened the door. He let Bobby go in first.

"Mom?" he called.

But there was no answer. They were probably still asleep. Ben found some dog food in the cabinet and pulled the bag out. He spilled on the floor when he filled Bobby's tray. He had no idea how much the dog needed, so he made sure to give him enough, and poured till the bowl overflowed. Ben found a garbage bag under the sink and had removed some of the bottles, when Bobby suddenly started growling. The dog ran to the bottom of the stairs and barked. Ben found this to be strange. It was very unlike Bobby to act this way.

"What's the matter, boy? Are Mom and Dad awake?"

The dog kept barking and growling.

"Stop it!" Ben yelled, knowing how much his dad hated it when Bobby barked. "Bad dog."

But Bobby didn't stop. He moved closer and closer to the stairs and kept barking until the dog finally ran up the stairs.

"No! Bobby!" Ben yelled. "Come back down here!"

Ben stared up the stairs after the dog, wondering if he dared to go up there. His dad always got so mad if he went upstairs when they were sleeping. He wasn't allowed up there until they got out of bed. But, if he found Bobby up there, his dad would get really mad. Probably talk about getting rid of him again.

He's my best friend. Don't take my friend away.

"Bobby," he whispered. "Come back down here."

Ben's heart was racing in his chest. There wasn't a sound coming from upstairs. Ben held his breath, not knowing what to do. The last thing he wanted on a day like today was to make his dad angry. He expected his dad to start yelling any second now.

Oh no, what if he jumps into their bed? Dad is going to get so mad. He's gonna get real mad at Bobby.

"Bobby?" Ben whispered a little louder.

There was movement on the stairs, the black lab peeked his head out, then ran down the stairs.

"There you are," Ben said with relief. Bobby ran past him and sprang up on the couch.

"What do you have in your mouth? Not one of mom's shoes again."

It didn't look like it was big enough to be a shoe. Ben walked closer, thinking if it was a pair of Mommy's panties again, then the dog was dead. He reached down and grabbed the dog's mouth, then opened it and pulled out whatever it was. He looked down with a small shriek at what had come out of the dog's mouth. He felt nauseated, like the time when he had the stomach-bug and spent the entire night in the bathroom. Only this was worse.

It's a finger. A finger wearing Mommy's ring!

4

JANUARY 2015

"Hit the road, Jack, and don't you come back no more no more no more."

The children's voices were screaming more than singing on the bus. I preferred *Wheels on the Bus,* but the kids thought it was oh so fun, since my name was Jack and I was actually driving the bus. I had volunteered to drive them to the Brevard Zoo for their field trip today. Two of the children, the pretty blonde twins in the back named Abigail and Austin, were mine. A boy and a girl. Just started Kindergarten six months ago. I could hardly believe how fast time passed. Everybody told me it would, but still. It was hard to believe.

I was thirty-five and a single dad of three children. My wife, Arianna, ran out on us four years ago…when the twins were almost two years old. It was too much, she told me. She couldn't cope with the children or me. She especially had a hard time taking care of Emily. Emily was my ex-partner's daughter. My ex-partner, Lisa, was shot on duty ten years ago during a chase in downtown Miami. The shooter was never captured, and it haunted me daily. I took Emily in after her mother died. What else could I have done? I felt guilty for what had happened to her mother. I was supposed to have protected my partner. Plus, the girl didn't know her father. Lisa never told anyone who he was; she didn't have any of her parents or siblings left, except for a homeless brother who was in no condition to take care of a child. So, I got custody and decided to give Emily the best life I could. She was six when I took her in, sixteen now, and at an age where it was hard for anyone to love you, besides your mom and dad. I tried hard to be both for her. Not always with much success. The fact was, I had no idea what it was like to be a black teenage girl.

Personally, I believed Arianna had depression after the birth of the twins, but she never let me close enough to talk about it. She cried for months after the twins were born, then one day out of the blue, she told me she had to go. That she couldn't stay or it would end up killing her. I cried and begged her to stay, but there was nothing I could do. She had made up her mind. She was going back upstate, and that was all I needed to know. I shouldn't look for her, she said.

"Are you coming back?" I asked, my voice breaking. I couldn't believe anyone would leave her own children.

"I don't know, Jack."

"But…The children? They need you? They need their mother?"

"I can't be the mother you want me to be, Jack. I'm just not cut out for it. I'm sorry."

Then she left. Just like that. I had no idea how to explain it to the kids, but somehow I did. As soon as they started asking questions, I told them their mother had left and that I believed she was coming back one day. Some, maybe a lot of people, including my mother, might have told me it was insane to tell them that she might be coming back, but that's what I did. I couldn't bear the thought of them growing up with the knowledge that their own mother didn't want them. I couldn't bear for Emily to know that she was part of the reason why Arianna had left us, left the twins motherless. I just couldn't. I had to leave them with some sort of hope. And maybe I needed to believe it too. I needed to believe that she hadn't just abandoned us...that she had some stuff she needed to work out and soon she would be back. At least for the twins. They needed their mother and asked for her often. It was getting harder and harder for me to believe she was coming back for them. But I still said she would.

And there they were.

On the back seat of the bus, singing along with their classmates, happier than most of them. Mother or no mother, I had provided a good life for them in our little town of Cocoa Beach. As a detective working for the Brevard County Sheriff's Office, working their homicide unit, I had lots of spare time and they had their grandparents close by. They received all the love in the world from me and their grandparents, who loved them to death (and let them get away with just about anything).

Some might think they were spoiled brats, but to me they were the love of my life, the light, the...the...

What the heck were they doing in the back?

I hit the brakes a little too hard at the red light. All the kids on the bus fell forwards. The teacher, Mrs. Allen, whined and held on to her purse.

"Abigail and Austin!" I thundered through the bus. "Stop that right now!"

The twins grinned and looked at one another, then continued to smear chocolate on each other's faces. Chocolate from those small boxes with Nutella and sticks you dipped in it. Boxes their grandmother had given them for snack, even though I told her it had to be healthy.

"Now!" I yelled.

"Sorry, Dad," they yelled in unison.

"Well...wipe that off or..."

I never made it any further before the phone in my pocket vibrated. I pulled it out and started driving again as the light turned green.

"Ryder. We need you. I spoke with Ron and he told me you would be assisting us. We desperately need your help."

It was the head of the Cocoa Beach Police Department. Weasel, we called her. I didn't know why. Maybe it had to do with the fact that her name was Weslie Seal. Maybe it was just because she kind of looked like a weasel because her body was long and slender, but her legs very short. Ron Harper was the county sheriff and my boss.

"Yes? When?"

"Now."

"But...I'm..."

"This is big. We need you now."

"If you say so. I'll get there as fast as I can," I said, and turned off towards the entrance to the zoo. The kids all screamed with joy when they saw the sign. Mrs. Allen shushed them.

"What, are you running a day-care now? Not that I have the time to care. Everything is upside down around here. We have a dead body. I'll text you the address. Meet you there."

5

APRIL 1984

Annie was getting ready. She was putting on make-up with her room-mate Julia, while listening to Michael Jackson's *Thriller* and singing into their hairbrushes. They were nineteen, in college, and heading for trouble, as Annie's father always said.

Annie wanted to be a teacher.

"Are you excited?" Julia asked. "You think he's going to be there?"

"He," was Tim. He was the talk of the campus and the guy they all desired. He was tall, blond, and a quarterback. He was perfect. And he had his eye on Annie.

"I hope so," Annie said, and put on her jacket with the shoulder pads. "He asked me to come; he'd better be."

She looked at her friend, wondering why Tim hadn't chosen Julia instead. She was much prettier.

"Shall we?" Julia asked and opened the door. They were both wearing heavy make-up and acid-washed jeans.

Annie was nervous as they walked to the party. She had never been to a party in a fraternity house before. She had been thrilled when Tim came up to her in the library where she hung out most of the time and told her there was a party at the house and asked if she was going to come.

"Sure," she had replied, while blushing.

"This is it," Julia said, as they approached the house. Kids a few years older than them were hanging out on the porch, while loud music spilled out through the open windows. Annie had butterflies in her stomach as they went up the steps to the front of the house and entered, elbowing themselves through the crowd.

The noise was intense. People were drinking and smoking everywhere. Some were already making out on a couch. And it wasn't even nine o'clock yet.

"Let's get something to drink," Julia yelled through the thick clamor. "Have you loosen up a little."

Julia came back with two cups, and...Tim. "Look who I found," she said. "He was asking for you."

Annie grabbed the plastic cup and didn't care what it contained; she gulped it down in such a hurry she forgot to breathe. Tim was staring at her with that handsome smile of his. Then, he leaned over, put his hand on her shoulder, and whispered. "Glad you came."

Annie blushed and felt warmth spread through her entire body from the palm of Tim's hand on her shoulder. She really liked him. She really, really liked him.

"It's very loud in here. Do you want to go somewhere?" he asked.

Annie knew she wasn't the smartest among girls. Her mother had always told her so. She knew Tim, who was pre-med, would never be impressed with her conversational skills or her wits. If she was to dazzle him, it had to be in another way.

"Sure," she said.

"Let me get us some drinks first," Tim said and disappeared.

Julia smiled and grabbed Annie's shoulders. "You got him, girl." Then she corrected Annie's hair and wiped a smear of mascara from under her eyes.

"There. Now you're perfect. Remember. Don't think. You always overthink everything. Just be you. Just go with the flow, all right? Laugh at his jokes, but not too hard. Don't tell him too much about yourself; stay mysterious. And, whatever you do…don't sleep with him. You hear me? He won't respect you if you jump into bed with him right away. You have to play hard to get."

Annie stared at Julia. She had never had sex with anyone before, and she certainly wasn't going to now. Not yet. She had been saving herself for the right guy, and maybe Tim was it, but she wasn't going to decide that tonight. She didn't even want to.

"I'd never do that," she said with a scoff. "I'm not THAT stupid."

6

JANUARY 2015

Weasel was standing outside the house as I drove up and parked the school bus on the street. The house on West Bay Drive was blocked by four police cars and lots of police tape. I saw several of my colleagues walking around in the yard. Weasel spotted me and approached. She was wearing tight black jeans, a belt with a big buckle, a white shirt, and black blazer. She looked to be in her thirties, but I knew she had recently turned forty.

"What the...?" she said with a grin, looking at the bus. She had that raspy rawness to her voice, and I always wondered if she could sing. I pictured her as a country singer. She gave out that tough vibe.

"Don't ask," I said. "What have we got?"

"Homicide," Weasel answered. "Victim is female. Laura Bennett, thirty-two, Mom of Ben, five years old. The husband's name is Brandon Bennett."

My heart dropped. I knew the boy. He was in the twins' class. I couldn't believe it. I had moved to Cocoa Beach from Miami in 2008 and never been called out to a homicide in my own town. Our biggest problems around here were usually tourists on spring break jumping in people's pools and Jacuzzis and leaving beer cans, or the youngsters having bonfires on the beach and burning people's chairs and leaving trash.

But, murder? That was a first for me in Cocoa Beach. I had been called out to drug related homicides in the beachside area before, but that was mostly further down south in Satellite Beach and Indialantic, but never this far up north.

"It's bad," Weasel said. "I have close to no experience with this type of thing, but you do. We need all your Miami-experience now. Show me what you've got."

I nodded and followed her into the house. It was located on a canal leading to the Banana River, like most of the houses on the back side of the island. The house had a big pebble-coated pool area with two waterfalls, a slide, and a spa overlooking the river. The perfect setting for Florida living, the real estate ad would say. With the huge palm trees, it looked like true paradise. Until you stepped inside.

The inside was pure hell.

It was a long time since I had been on a murder scene, but the Weasel was right. I was the only one with lots of experience in this field. I spent eight years in downtown Miami, covering Overtown, the worst neighborhood in the town, as part of the homicide unit. My specialty was the killer's psychology. I was a big deal back then. But when I met Arianna and she became pregnant with the twins, I was done. It was suddenly too dangerous. We left Miami to get away from it. We moved to Cocoa Beach, where my parents lived, to be closer to my family and to get away from murder.

Now, it had followed me here. It made me feel awful. I hated to see the town's innocence go like this.

My colleagues from the Cocoa Beach Police Department greeted me with nods as we walked through the living room, overlooking the yard with the pool. I knew all of them. They seemed a little confused. For most of them, it was a first. Officer Joel Hall looked pale.

"Joel was first man here," Weasel said.

"How are you doing, Joel?" I asked.

"Been better."

"So, tell me what happened."

Joel sniffled and wiped his nose on his sleeve.

"We got a call from the boy. He told us his mother had been killed. He found her finger...well, the dog had it in his mouth. He didn't dare to go upstairs. He called 911 immediately. I was on patrol close by, so I drove down here."

"So, what did you find?"

"The boy and the dog were waiting outside the house. He was hysterical, kept telling me his parents were dead. Then, he showed me the finger. I tried to calm him down and tell him I would go look and to stay outside. I walked up and found the mother..." Joel sniffled again. He took in a deep breath.

"Take your time, Joel," I said, and put my hand on his shoulder. Joel finally caved in and broke down.

"You better see it with your own eyes," Weasel said. "But brace yourself."

I followed her up the stairs of the house, where the medical examiners were already taking samples.

"The kid said his parents were dead. What about the dad?" I asked. "You only said one homicide."

"The dad's fine. But, hear this," Weasel said. "He claims he was asleep the entire time. He's been taken to the hospital to see a doctor. He kept claiming he felt dizzy and had blurred vision. I had to have a doctor look at him before we talk to him. The boy is with him. Didn't want to leave his side. The dog is there too. Jim and Marty took them there. I don't want him to run. He's our main suspect so far."

We walked down the hallway till we reached the bedroom.

"Brace yourself," Weasel repeated, right before we walked inside.

I sucked in my breath. Then I froze.

"It looks like he was dismembering her," Weasel said. "He cut off all the fingers on her right hand, one by one, then continued on to the toes on her foot."

I felt disgusted by the sight. I held a hand to cover my mouth, not because it smelled, but because I always became sick to my stomach when facing a dead body. Especially one that was mutilated. I never got used to it. I kneeled next to the woman lying on the floor. I examined her face and eyes, lifted her eyelids, then looked closely at her body.

"There's hardly any blood. No bruises either," I said. "I say she was strangled first, then he did the dismembering. My guess is he was disturbed. He was about to cut her into bits and pieces, but he stopped. "I sniffed the body and looked at the Weasel, who seemed disgusted by my motion. "The kill might have happened in the shower. She has been washed recently. Maybe he drowned her."

I walked into the bathroom and approached the tub. I ran a finger along the sides. "Look." I showed her my finger. "There's still water on the sides. It's been used recently."

"So, you think she was killed in the bathtub? Strangulation, you say? But there are no marks on her neck or throat?"

"Look at her eyes. Petechiae. Tiny red spots due to ruptured capillaries. They are a signature injury of strangulation. She has them under the eyelids. He didn't use his hands. He was being gentle."

Weasel looked appalled. "Gentle? How can you say he was gentle? He cut off her fingers?"

"Yes, but look how methodical he was. All the parts are intact. Not a bruise on any of them. Not a drop of blood. They are all placed neatly next to one another. It's a declaration of love."

Weasel looked confused. She grumbled. "I don't see much love in any of all this, that's for sure. All I see is a dead woman, who someone tried to chop up. And now I want you to find out who did it."

I chuckled. "So, the dad tells us he was sleeping?" I asked.

Weasel shrugged. "Apparently, he was drunk last night. They had friends over. It got a little heavy, according to the neighbors. Loud music and loud voices. But that isn't new with these people."

"On a Sunday night in a nice neighborhood like this?" I asked, surprised.

"Apparently."

"It's a big house. Right on the river. Snug Harbor is one of the most expensive neighborhoods around here. What do the parents do for a living?"

"Nothing, I've been told. They live off the family's money. The deceased's father was a very famous writer. He died ten years ago. The kids have been living off of the inheritance and the royalties for years since."

"Anyone I know, the writer?"

"Probably," she said. "A local hero around here. John Platt."

"John Platt?" I said. "I've certainly heard of him. I didn't know he used to live around here. Wasn't he the guy who wrote all those thriller-novels that were made into movies later on?"

"Yes, that was him. He has sold more than 100 million books worldwide. His books are still topping the bestseller lists."

"Didn't he recently publish a new book or something?"

Weasel nodded. "They found an old unpublished manuscript of his on his computer, which they published. I never understood how those things work, but I figure they think, if he wrote it, then it's worth a lot of money even if he trashed it."

I stared at the dead halfway-dismembered body on the floor, then back at the Weasel.

I sighed. "I guess we better talk to this heavily sleeping dad first."

7

JANUARY 2015

"Who was that guy you talked to last night?"

Joe walked into the kitchen. Shannon was cutting up oranges to make juice. She sensed he was right behind her, but she didn't turn to look at him. Last night was still in her head. The humming noise of the voices, the music, the laughter. Her head was hurting from a little too much alcohol. His question made everything inside of her freeze.

"Who do you mean?" she asked. "I talked to a lot of people. That was kind of the idea with the party after my concert. For me to meet with the press and important people in the business. That's the way it always is. You know how it goes. It's a big part of my job."

He put his hand on her shoulder. A shiver ran up her spine. She closed her eyes.

Not now. Please not now.

"Look at me when you're talking to me," he said.

She took in a deep breath, then put on a smile; the same smile she used when the press asked her to pose for pictures, the same smile she put on for her manager, her record label, and her friends when they asked her about the bruises on her back, followed by the sentence:

"Just me being clumsy again."

Shannon turned and looked at Joe. His eyes were black with fury. Her body shrunk and her smile froze.

"I saw the way you were looking at that guy. Don't you think I saw that?" Joe asked. "You know what I think? I think you like going to these parties they throw in your honor. I think you enjoy all the men staring at you, wishing you were theirs, wanting to fuck your brains out. I see it in their eyes and I see it in yours as well. You like it."

It was always the same. Joe couldn't stand the fact that Shannon was the famous one...that she was the one everyone wanted to talk to, and after a party like the one yesterday, he always lost his temper with her. Because he felt left out, because there was no one looking at him, talking to him, asking him questions with interest. He hated the fact that Shannon was the one with a career, when all he had ever dreamt of was to be singing in sold out stadiums like she did.

They had started out together. Each with just a guitar under their arm, working small clubs and bars in Texas, then later they moved on to Nashville, where country musicians were made. They played the streets together, and then got small gigs in bars, and later small concert venues around town. But when a record label contacted them one day after a concert, they were only interested in her. They only wanted Shannon King. Since then, Joe had been living in the shadow of his wife, and that didn't become him well. For years, she had made excuses for him, telling herself he was going through a rough time; he was just hurting because he wasn't going anywhere with his music. The only thing Joe had going for him right now was the fact that he was stronger than Shannon.

But as the years had passed, it was getting harder and harder for her to come up with new excuses, new explanations. Especially now that they had a child together. A little girl who was beginning to ask questions.

"Joe...I...I don't know what you're talking about. I talked to a lot of people last night. I'm tired and now I really want to get some breakfast."

"Did you just take a tone with me. Did ya'? Am I so insignificant in your life that you don't even talk to me with respect, huh? You don't even look at me when we're at your precious after party. Nobody cares about me. Everyone just wants to talk to the *biiig* star, Shannon King," he said, mocking her.

"You're being ridiculous."

"Am I? Did you even think about me once last night? Did you? I left at eleven-thirty. You never even noticed. You never even texted me and asked where I was."

Shannon blushed. He was right. She hadn't thought about him even once. She had been busy answering questions from the press and talking about her tour. Everyone had been pulling at her; there simply was no time to think about him. Why couldn't he understand that?

"I thought so," Joe said. Then, he slapped her.

Shannon went stumbling backward against the massive granite counter. She hurt her back in the fall. Shannon whimpered, then got up on her feet again with much effort. Her cheek burned like hell. A little blood ran from the corner of her mouth. She wiped it off.

Careful what you say, Shannon. Careful not to upset him further. Remember what happened last time. He's not well. He is hurting. Careful not to hurt him any more.

But she knew it was too late. She knew once he crossed that line into that area where all thinking ceased to exist, it was too late. She could appeal to his sensitivity as much as she wanted to. She could try and explain herself and tell him she was sorry, but it didn't help. If anything, it only made everything worse.

His eyes were bulging and his jaws clenched. His right eye had that tick in it that only showed when he was angry.

You got to get out of here.

"Joe, please, I…"

A fist throbbed through the air and smashed into her face.

Quick. Run for the phone.

She could see it. It was on the breakfast bar. She would have to spring for it. Shannon jumped to the side and managed to avoid his next fist, then slipped on the small rug on the kitchen floor, got back up in a hurry, and rushed to reach out for the phone.

Call 911. Call the police.

Her legs were in the air and she wasn't running anymore. He had grabbed her by the hair, and now he was pulling her backwards. He yanked her towards him, and she screamed in pain, cursing her long blonde hair that she used to love so much…that the world loved and put on magazine covers.

"You cheating lying bitch!" he screamed, while pulling her across the floor.

He lifted her up, then threw her against the kitchen counter. It blew out the air from her lungs. She couldn't scream anymore. She was panting for air and wheezing for him to stop. She was bleeding from her nose. Joe came closer, then leaned over her and, with his hand, he corrected his hair. His precious hair that had always meant so much to him, that he was always fixing and touching to make sure it was perfect, which it ironically never was.

"No one disrespects me. Do you hear me? Especially not you. You're a nobody. Do you understand? You would be nothing if it wasn't for me," he yelled, then lifted his clenched fist one more time. When it smashed into Shannon's face again and again, she finally let herself drift into a darkness so deep she couldn't feel anything anymore.

8

JANUARY 2015

"Hi there. Ben, is it?" I asked.

The boy was sitting next to his dad in the hospital bed, the dog sleeping by his feet.

"He won't leave his dad's side," Marty said.

Ben looked up at me with fear in his eyes. "It's okay, Ben," I said, and kneeled in front of him. "We can talk here."

"I know you," Ben said. "You're Austin and Abigail's dad."

"That's right. And you're in their class. I remember you. Say, weren't you supposed to be at the zoo today?"

Ben nodded with a sad expression.

"Well, there'll be other times," I said. I paused while Ben looked at his father, who was sleeping.

"He's completely out cold," Marty said. "He was complaining that he couldn't control his arms and legs, had spots before his eyes, and he felt dizzy and nauseated. Guess it was really heavy last night."

I looked at the very pale dad. "Or maybe it was something else," I said.

"What do you mean?"

I looked closer at the dad.

"Did you talk to him?"

"Only a few words. When I asked about last night, he kept saying he didn't remember what happened, that he didn't know where he was. He kept asking me what time it was. Even after I had just told him."

"Hm."

"What?" Marty asked.

"Did they run his blood work?" I asked.

"No. I told them it wasn't necessary. He was just hung over. The doctor looked at him quickly and agreed. We agreed to let him to sleep it off. He seemed like he was still drunk when he talked to us."

"Is my dad sick, Mr. Ryder?" Ben asked.

I looked at the boy and smiled. "No, son, but I am afraid your dad has been poisoned."

"Poisoned?" Marty asked. "What on earth do you mean?"

"Dizziness, confusion, blurry vision, difficulty talking, nausea, difficulty controlling your movements all are symptoms of Rohypnol poisoning. Must have been ingested to have this big of an affect. Especially with alcohol."

"Roofied?" Marty laughed. "Who on earth in their right mind would give a grown man a rape drug?"

"Someone who wanted to kill him and his wife," I said.

I walked into the hallway and found a nurse and asked her to make sure they tested Brandon Bennett for the drug in his blood. Then, I called the medical examiner and told them to check the wife's blood as well. Afterwards, I returned to talk to Ben.

"So, Ben, I know this is a difficult time for you, but I would be really happy if you could help me out by talking a little about last night. Can you help me out here?"

Ben wiped his eyes and looked at me. His face was swollen from crying. Then he nodded. I opened my arms. "Come here, buddy. You look like you could use a good bear hug."

Ben hesitated, then looked at his dad, who was still out cold, before he finally gave in and let me hug him. I held him in my arms, the way I held my own children when they were sad. The boy finally cried.

"It's okay," I whispered. "Your dad will be fine."

My words felt vague compared to what the little boy had seen this morning, how his world had been shaken up. His dad was probably going to be fine, but he would never see his mother again, and the real question was whether the boy would ever be fine again?

He wept in my arms for a few minutes, then pulled away and wiped his nose on his sleeve. "Do you promise to catch the guy that killed my mother?" he asked.

I sighed. "I can promise I'll do my best. How about that?"

Ben thought about it for a little while, then nodded with a sniffle.

"Okay. What do you want to know?" he asked.

"Who came to your house last night? I heard your parents had guests. Who were they?"

9

APRIL 1984

Tim took Annie down to the lake behind campus, where they sat down. The grass was moist from the sprinklers. Annie felt self-conscious with the way Tim stared at her. It was a hot night out. The cicadas were singing; Annie was sweating in her small dress. Her skin felt clammy.

Tim finally broke the silence.

"Has anyone ever told you how incredibly beautiful you are?"

Annie's head was spinning from her drink. The night was intoxicating, the sounds, the smell, the moist air hugging her. She shook her head. Her eyes stared at the grass. She felt her cheeks blushing.

"No."

"Really?" Tim said. "I find that very hard to believe."

Annie giggled, then sipped her drink. She really liked Tim. She could hardly believe she was really here with him.

"Look at the moon," he said and pointed.

It was a full moon. It was shining almost as bright as daylight. Its light hit the lake. Annie took in a deep breath, taking in the moment.

"It's beautiful," she said with a small still voice. She was afraid of talking too much, since he would only realize she wasn't smart, and then he might regret being with her.

Just go with the flow.

"I loathe Florida," Tim said. "I hate these warm nights. I hate how sweaty I always am. I'm especially sick of Orlando. When I'm done here, I'm getting out of this state. I wanna go up north. Don't you?"

Annie shrugged. She had lived all her life in Florida. Thirty minutes north of Orlando, to be exact. Born and raised in Windermere. Her parents still lived there, and that was where she was planning on going back once she had her degree. Annie had never thought about going anywhere else.

"I guess it's nice up north as well," she said, just to please him.

Tim laughed, then looked at her with those intense eyes once again. It made her uncomfortable. But part of her liked it as well. A big part.

"Can I kiss you?" he asked.

Annie blushed. She really wanted him to. Then she nodded. Tim smiled, then leaned over and put his lips on top of hers. Annie felt the dizziness from the drink. It was buzzing in her head. The kiss made her head spin, and when Tim pressed her down on the moist grass, she let him. He crawled on top of her, and with deep moans kept kissing her lips, then her cheeks, her ears, and her neck. Annie felt like laughing because it tickled so much, but she held it back to not ruin anything. Tim liked her and it made her happy.

"Boy, you're hot," he said, groaning, as he kissed her throat and moved further down her body. He grinned and started to open her dress, taking one button at a time. Annie felt insecure. What was he going to do next?

Tim pulled the dress open and looked at her bra, then he ripped it off.

"Ouch," Annie said. She tried to cover her breasts with her arms, but Tim soon grabbed them and pulled them to her sides. He held her down while kissing her breasts. He groaned while sucking on her nipples. Annie wasn't sure if she liked it or not. He was being a little rough, and she was afraid of going too far with him.

Whatever you do, don't sleep with him. No matter what.

"Stop," she mumbled, when he pulled the dress off completely and grabbed her panties. Tim stopped. He stared at Annie. She felt bad. Had she scared him away? Was he ever going to see her again if she didn't let him?

No matter what.

No. She wasn't ready for this. She had saved herself. This wasn't how it was supposed to happen. Not like this. Not here.

"I want to go home," Annie said.

Tim smiled and tilted his head, then leaned over and whispered in her ear. "Not yet, sweetheart, not yet."

He stroked her face gently and kissed her cheeks, while she fought and tried to get him off her body. In the distance, she heard voices, and soon she felt hands on her body, hands touching her, hands slapping her face. She felt so dizzy and everything became a blur of faces, laughing voices, cheering voices, hands everywhere, groping her, touching her, hurting her. And then the pain followed.

The excruciating pain.

10

JANUARY 2015

Brandon Bennett was still out cold when I had to leave the hospital. I decided to wait to interrogate him till later. Ben had told me that he had been asleep, so he hadn't seen who was at the house, but there were two of his parents' neighbors who usually came over to drink with his mom and dad. I got the names and called for both of them to come into the station in the afternoon. Meanwhile, I had to drive back to the zoo to pick up the kids and get them back to their school.

"Daddy!" my kids yelled when I opened the doors to the school bus and they stormed in, screaming with joy. Both of them clung to my neck.

"How was the zoo?" I asked.

"So much fun!" Abigail exclaimed. She was the most outgoing of the two, and often the one who spoke for them. I had a feeling Austin was the thinker, the one who would turn out to be a genius some day. Well, maybe not exactly a genius, but there was something about him. Abigail was the one who came up with all their naughty plans, and she always got Austin in on them.

"Good. I'm glad," I said and smooched their cheeks loudly.

"You would have loved it, Dad," Abigail continued. "You should have come. What was so important anyway?"

I exhaled and kissed her again, then let go of her. "Just some work thing. Nothing to worry about."

The twins looked at each other. Abigail placed her hands on her hips and looked at me with her head tilted.

"What?" I asked.

"You only say for us to not worry if there is actually something to worry about," Abigail said. "Am I right?" She looked at Austin, who nodded.

"She's right, Dad."

I smiled. "Well, it is nothing smart little noses like yours should get into, so get in the back of the bus with your friends and sit down. We're leaving now."

Abigail grumbled something, then grabbed her brother's shirt and they walked to the back. The bus gave a deep sigh when I closed the doors and we took off.

The atmosphere on the bus driving back was loud and very cheerful. Loudest of all were my twins, but this time I didn't mind too much. After the morning I had spent with a dead body and a poor kid who had lost his mother, I was just so pleased that my kids were still happy and innocent. They didn't look at me with that empty stare in their eyes, the one where you know they'll never trust the world again. That broken look that made them appear so much older than they were.

"Grandma and Grandpa will pick you up," I said, as I dropped them off at Roosevelt Elementary School.

"Yay!" they both exclaimed.

I told their teacher as well, then parked the bus and gave the keys back to the front office.

"Thank you so much for helping out today," Elaine at the desk said. "It's always wonderful when the parents get involved."

"Anytime," I said.

I walked to my car, a red Jeep Convertible. I got in and drove to the station with the top down. I bought my favorite sandwich at Juice 'N Java Café, called Cienna. It had a Portobello mushroom, yellow tomato, goat cheese arugula, and pesto on Pugliese bread. I figured I had earned it after the morning I had.

The police station was located inside of City Hall, right in the heart of Cocoa Beach. I knew the place well, even though I was usually located at the sheriff's offices in Rockledge. Cocoa Beach was my town, and every time they needed a detective, I was the one they called for. Even if they were cases that didn't involve homicide. As I entered through the glass doors, Weasel came towards me. Two officers flanked her.

"Going out for lunch?" I asked.

"Yes. I see you've already gotten yours," she said, nodding at my bag with my sandwich from the café.

"I'm expecting two of the neighbors in for questioning in a short while. Any news I should know about?" I asked.

Weasel sighed. "The ME has taken the body in for examination. They expect to have the cause of death within a few hours, they say. They're still working on the house."

"Any fingerprints so far?"

"Lots. We asked around a little and heard the same story from most of the neighbors. The Bennetts were a noisy bunch. Nothing that has ever been reported, but the wife and husband fought a lot, one neighbor told us. He said they yelled and screamed at each other when they got drunk. He figured the husband finally had enough. I guess it sounds plausible. He killed her, then panicked and tried to dismember her body to get rid of it. But the dog interrupted him. He decided to pretend he had been asleep through the whole thing. When we arrived, the dad was asleep when Joel went up, but he might have pretended to be. Joel said he seemed out of it, though. Might just be a good actor."

"It's all a lot of theories so far," I said with a deep exhale. It was going to be a long day for me. I was so grateful I had my parents nearby.

I grew up in Ft. Lauderdale, further down south, but when I left for college, my parents wanted to try something new. They bought a motel by the beach in Cocoa Beach a few years after I left the house. The place was a haven for the kids. They never missed me while they were there. That made it easier for me to work late.

"I've cleared an office for you," Weasel said. "We're glad to have you here to help us."

I put a hand on her broad shoulder. "Likewise. I'll hold down the fort. Enjoy your lunch."

END OF EXCERPT...

CLICK HERE TO ORDER

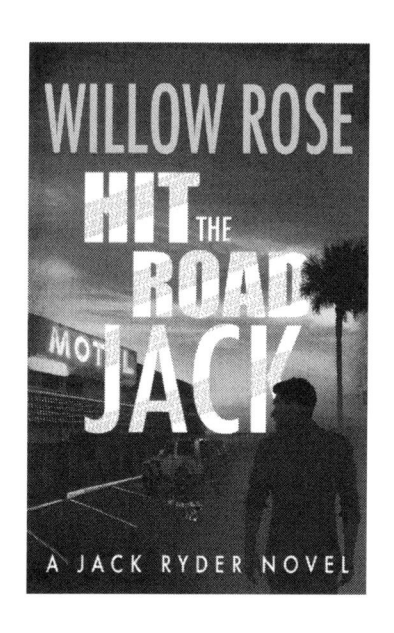

GRAB YOUR COPY NOW HERE:
https://www.amazon.com/Hit-Road-Jack-wickedly-suspenseful-ebook/dp/B00V9525BC

Printed in Great Britain
by Amazon